**"Emma,"** Alex said, pinning her against the wall in a spectacularly graffitied alley, the walls an ever-changing work of art, when he could bear it no more.

"I have to tell you. I really don't care about seeing the city. I just want to get you back in my bed."

He could barely believe that he wanted to take her back home. Sending her on her way was the smarter plan. But how smart was it really to deny himself? Emma knew the score. This wasn't about feelings or a relationship. It was just sex.

"Give me the weekend. I promise you won't regret it." His voice was low and rough. He could see in her eyes that she knew just how aroused he was and, with his body against hers, she could feel it.

"I want that too," she breathed.

"What I said before still stands. This doesn't change things."

"I know that." She grinned. "I don't want it to."

**Bella Mason** has been a bookworm from an early age. She has been regaling people with stories from the time she discovered she could hold the dinner table hostage with her reimagined fairy tales. After earning a degree in journalism, she rekindled her love of writing and now writes full-time. When she isn't imagining dashing heroes and strong heroines, she can be found exploring Melbourne, burying her nose in a book or lusting after fast cars.

*This is Bella Mason's debut book for Harlequin Presents.*

*We hope that you enjoy it!*

# *Bella Mason*

---

## AWAKENED BY THE WILD BILLIONAIRE

HARLEQUIN
PRESENTS

Recycling programs for this product may not exist in your area.

ISBN-13: 978-1-335-73875-2

Awakened by the Wild Billionaire

Copyright © 2022 by Bella Mason

For questions and comments about the quality of this book, please contact us at CustomerService@Harlequin.com.

Harlequin Enterprises ULC
22 Adelaide St. West, 41st Floor
Toronto, Ontario M5H 4E3, Canada
www.Harlequin.com

Printed in U.S.A.

# AWAKENED BY THE WILD BILLIONAIRE

To my three cheerleaders for your endless support and my wonderful husband, without whom this book wouldn't exist.

# CHAPTER ONE

*DEEP BREATHS.*

Emma Brown ascended the stairs to the party venue, and as she entered the ballroom looked around the dimly lit, extravagantly decorated space hoping to find her best friend. She wanted to adjust her mask and flatten her cobalt dress for the hundredth time, but silently instructed herself to stop fidgeting.

She walked through the entrance, eyes searching for her friend's tall frame amongst the sea of ballgown-clad women. There were masks of every colour, style and shape wherever she looked. Everyone seemed to be glittering in their adornments, and every hand was accessorised with an elegant glass of champagne.

Crystal chandeliers hung from the draped ceiling, reflecting light in all directions. Emma looked out at the wall of glass, a small smile playing on her lips as she walked, admiring the thousands of golden fairy lights as their glow danced on the surface of a pool. This hotel was always beautiful. She loved how the city rose up around it. There were very few places she loved as much as Melbourne.

She was so completely bewitched by her surroundings that she paid no attention to where she was walking until she hit a very solid wall that knocked the breath out of her. A strong arm wrapped around her waist, steadying her.

'Oh! Ex-excuse me,' she stuttered.

'Are you okay?' a deep, resonating voice asked.

She was mesmerised, both by the crisp English accent and the piercing sky-blue eyes that bore down into hers, and her stomach was doing somersaults. Emma could feel pure heat radiating from the hand on her back, but she wasn't sure of anything in that moment apart from the fact her heart was going at a million miles an hour.

'Um…yeah… Sorry about that.' She laughed nervously as she righted herself. 'Enjoy your evening,' she murmured as she walked away from him, blushing furiously.

Emma looked back over her shoulder at the tuxedo-clad man in his simple black mask and was delighted to see he was still watching her. She turned around and spotted her sisters, who had already started mingling and were nodding to her to join them, but Emma was immensely thankful that Hannah was nearby, waving her over.

Hannah, her best friend, roommate and eternal saviour, was the only reason Emma had agreed to attend this charity masquerade. It had been Emma's twenty-eighth birthday the day before, and Hannah had thought they could extend the celebration. And right now, as she once again stole a glance at the handsome stranger, she was very happy she had agreed.

'Hey! You look amazing!' Hannah gushed as she hugged her.

'Thanks…' Emma mumbled, fiddling with the fine silver filigree mask she wore. 'You're going to turn heads tonight.'

'And beds.' Hannah chuckled darkly, twirling a lock of red hair around her finger.

'You're terrible.'

'Probably.' Hannah handed her a tall flute of bubbly. 'I think you're going to need that in you before your sisters come over here.'

'Got anything stronger?'

'Left the poison in my other bag,' Hannah deadpanned. 'So, who's the dreamboat that keeps looking at you?'

'I'm pretty sure that's Lord Alexander Hastings,' Emma whispered.

'Pretty sure?'

'The mask adds some doubt.'

'Why don't you go over there and introduce yourself and eliminate the doubt? Seriously, he looks like he'd be interested.'

'I very much doubt that—especially after I nearly bowled him over.'

Hannah laughed. 'You're an idiot. And speaking of idiots… Lauren incoming.'

'Great.'

Emma and Hannah fixed polite smiles in place as the woman approached. Lauren, the eldest of her sisters, and by most accounts the most beautiful, was blessed in many ways. Tall, blonde, with hazel eyes with flecks of gold that could bewitch most. Eyes that her younger sister Maddison shared. Lauren had always made Emma feel plain. But perhaps her biggest blessing of all, was the unequivocal favour she enjoyed from their father.

'Hey, sis,' Emma greeted her. 'Where's Maddie?'

'Somewhere around here. You've made an effort, I see,' Lauren said haughtily.

But Emma wasn't listening. Her gaze was fixed on the man who seemed to be pulling at her on a primal level. He stood with one hand in his pocket as he spoke to the group of people around him. She could see the smirk on his face despite the dim lighting, and knew he was watching her as much as she watched him. Or maybe that was just wishful thinking.

Emma tried to ignore the waspish conversation between her best friend and her sister. And she was so absorbed in watching him she didn't notice when Maddison had joined them.

'Emma!' Lauren said impatiently.

That tore her attention back to her present company. 'I'm sorry—what?'

'Honestly! I asked you what made you come tonight? I thought you were staying home with the furball.' Lauren pinned an accusatory glare on Emma.

'I changed my mind. I had an invitation—just like you, Lauren.' Emma could feel the night plunging into a nightmare. Clearly it was a mistake to have come.

'Yes, well…just remember *I'm* here representing the company.'

Emma let out a breath of a laugh. 'I know that, Lauren. I'd never dream of stealing your thunder—especially when I can enjoy my Friday night while you have to work the room.'

'Guys, maybe we should go somewhere quieter,' Maddison interrupted, casting an apologetic gaze at Emma.

'There's no need, Maddie. We're just talking.' Lauren flicked her hair back, raising her flute of champagne to her lips.

The vast room was still humming with the sound of conversation. People everywhere were chatting and laughing and smiling. It seemed no one had even noticed her. Except one person, and he frowned as he watched the beaming smile vanish from Emma's face. She thought she caught his eye as she watched him walk away from the group of people he had been talking to.

'I think we should go and mingle,' Emma suggested, trying to defuse the tension. All she needed was time with Hannah and her mood would lift once again.

Unfortunately Lauren took Emma's arm and dragged her away. She must have noticed Emma staring at Alexander Hastings and decided she was going to do something about it.

'I couldn't agree more,' she said.

# CHAPTER TWO

ALEX SAW THE two women approach out of the corner of his eye as he nursed his whisky, and had to swallow down his disappointment that the intriguing brunette was not alone. He silently chastised himself for feeling anything,—after all, he'd barely interacted with her. It was ridiculous to feel anything.

But feel something he did. Whenever she set those blue-grey eyes on him. And every time he caught her staring…every time he'd seen her fidget. She was beguiling him and he had no idea why. Why should she hold any more appeal than the other mask-adorned women present?

When the two women finally reached him, he was rather put out that it wasn't she who spoke first.

'Mind if we join you?' the stunning blonde asked, in an overly flirtatious manner that set his teeth on edge. He had dealt with too many women like her in the past.

'Feel free.' He gestured to the single free chair which she sank onto, the slit in her dress falling open seductively. He fought the urge to roll his eyes. Instead, he offered up his own seat to the brunette, but before she could thank him the blonde interrupted.

'Lauren Brown,' she said, extending her hand. 'And this is my sister Emma.'

'Pleasure to meet you both.'

'Mmm…an English accent.' Lauren touched his arm. 'Are you new in town?' she continued.

'Fairly,' Alex replied with a forced smile.

'Well, why don't you ask me to dance and we can get better acquainted?'

Alex saw a muscle twitch in Emma's jaw and watched with fascination as she closed her eyes and took a deep breath. When she opened them he could tell she was visibly calmer. That was interesting.

'I think a dance is a lovely idea,' Alex replied. 'Emma, would you like to join me?' He fixed her with his penetrating stare, his hand outstretched, waiting.

Appearing to be completely shocked, she placed her hand in his. 'I would love to.'

Emma linked her arm with his as he led her to the dance floor. The last thing she noticed was the very sour look on her sister's face. There was nothing Emma could want that Lauren wouldn't have first.

She had no idea what music played as he swept her into his arms—she still could not believe that anyone would choose her over Lauren. That was definitely a first.

As his warm hand came to rest on her back she couldn't hold back the shiver that ran through her body. She moved effortlessly with him, almost as if she was magnetised to move with him. This was certainly an attraction she had never experienced before.

'I'm Alexander Hastings, by the way,' he said softly.

'I know. I think everyone in Melbourne knows. You've caused quite a stir.'

'Have I?'

He had. And it wasn't just because of his company. There were many pages and groups on social media dedicated to the appreciation of the thirty-two-year-old playboy billionaire, the son of an English Earl, and his good looks. In almost every picture he appeared with a different date. Every one of them tall, leggy. Polished. Now, being so close to him, she could see why.

She wanted to run her fingers over the stubble on his face, to kiss the sharpness of his jaw, to tug on the soft black hair cut in a short quiff. The look in the sky-blue eyes rimmed by thick dark lashes could set her aflame. It was both intense and predatory.

'I think you know you have.' She smiled.

'I do like the attention.'

He smirked, sliding his hand down to rest on the small of her back, pulling her closer and trapping her in his gaze. Never in her life had she wanted to be kissed so badly.

Alex watched as Emma bit her lip, and it made him want to take her right there in the middle of this ball-room. He valued control and she was making that slip.

'I think we should get a drink,' he said, breaking the spell.

Even to his own ears he could hear how low his voice

had become. He plucked two flutes of champagne off a tray as a waiter walked by and led Emma out onto the pool terrace. She made a beeline for the railing, looking out at the city bathed in light against an inky sky.

'Isn't it beautiful?' There was a faraway look in her eyes.

'Unbelievably,' he said, looking down at her, and handed her a glass of the golden liquid.

A chill breeze blew, causing her to shiver slightly. He placed his own glass down and shrugged out of his jacket, draping it over her shoulders.

'Thank you.' She smiled.

That smile did things to him. How could he find her so mesmerising when he hadn't even seen all of her face yet?

Alex wanted to kiss her right then. It didn't matter that they were at a public event. It didn't matter that he had only known her for the better part of an hour. He would be gone by morning anyway.

'I love this city. Have you seen much of it?'

Emma's voice cut through his thoughts and he had to force himself back to reality.

'Not nearly enough,' he answered.

'Well, Alexander, maybe I'll show you around sometime.'

The promise caused a stirring in him. He joined her at the railing and never before had he so desperately wanted to leave a party with someone. The sparkle in her eye when she looked at him made him think that maybe she felt the same.

'Would you like to get a drink?' he asked.

'I thought we were having one right now.' She laughed—a musical chime.

'I was thinking about somewhere quieter with even better views.'

He bathed her in a crooked smile and Emma's stomach flipped. She wanted to taste that smile.

She had to bite down a giggle at the errant thought. She was usually cautious. She was never impulsive. But with his scent all around her, she was overwhelmed by his presence. Maybe it was time for a little fun.

'You know what? I'd love to.'

And there was that smile again.

They placed their glasses down on a nearby cocktail table and he led her out with his warm hand on the small of her back again. She felt the heat radiate through her.

On her way out, Emma caught the murderous look on Lauren's face and had to stifle an urge to laugh, feeling a crazy level of excitement.

Alex held open the door for her when they got down to the lobby, and they stepped out into the night air. Holding Emma's hand in his, he approached the valet and in no time at all a luxury black sedan pulled up in front of them. One of the sponsors for the night was a ride-share company, which had had all the guests driven to the venue. Emma was grateful. It allowed Alex to sit beside her after helping her in.

He gave the driver his address and Emma made to remove her mask. But he stopped her. 'Keep it on.'

Staring into his eyes, and seeing all the carnal promise they held, she let go of the ribbons keeping it in place. That smile was back as he gave her hand a squeeze and looked out of the window as the city lights flashed by on the way to his Port Melbourne penthouse. It gave her an opportunity to study his features without being seen.

Emma fought an urge to place her lips below his jaw. They were still in public, and she was nothing if not proper.

The car pulled up in front of his building and he held his hand out for her before shutting the door and leading her inside. Her heart thrummed in her chest when the doors to the elevator slid closed. Alex's arm wrapped around her waist, pulling her against his side, and his lips travelled along her neck. A sigh escaped her, and she felt as much as heard his chuckle.

A *ding* interrupted them, making her curse at how fast the elevator had ascended. With a cleared throat, and as much poise as she could muster, Emma followed him into his apartment.

## CHAPTER THREE

THE WIND WAS knocked out of her. He really had been telling the truth. Emma didn't even notice the rest of the apartment. The floor-to-ceiling windows called to her.

The view was magnificent. She slipped off his jacket, draping it over a large couch she didn't even look at as she made her way to appreciate it. She could see the silver and gold lights of the ferry alongside the pier, all the way out to sea. Then she realised just how *much* she could see, and figured the glass panes must wrap all the way around the two-storey apartment.

The ceilings were high, and she could only imagine how much light filled the space during the day. She was surrounded by glass and steel. It was such an immaculately neat, modern space, but still warm and inviting, and for whatever reason, she felt this could not be a more perfect home for Alex.

Emma felt his presence behind her and turned around to see him pull off his black mask, which he placed on the large coffee table.

Seeing his face, she instantly thought none of the pictures she had seen did him a shred of justice. He was undoubtedly the most beautiful man she had ever seen.

Before she'd even registered the pull his eyes had on her he was already standing before her, his hands going to her hair. With a gentle tug on the ribbons, the bow fell away and the silver mask came loose.

'I wanted to do that all night,' Alex said.

He placed it beside his, and when he turned back to her a slow, delicious smile curved his mouth.

The thought that it should be criminal to look so good occurred to her. And right then all she wanted to do was to run her fingers along his lips.

Alex watched her gaze travel to his mouth, followed by the soft touch of her fingers. It was heaven. He caught her hand, pressing a kiss to the pads of her fingers before drawing one into his mouth. Her breath left her in a sigh and she closed her eyes, shutting away her blue-grey gaze. He realised he wanted them back on him. He playfully nipped at her finger and her eyes flew open as she tried to pull back. But he gripped her finger between his exposed teeth.

The look on her face was caught somewhere between amusement and arousal, but he was about to tip that balance.

His hand went to her waist, drawing her against his body, while the other travelled up her arm, settling on the nape of her neck. He let her fingers fall from his mouth and instantly her hands were on his chest. Feeling the hard muscle beneath his shirt.

Their gazes caught. A moment passed eternally between them, before he leaned down, brushing his lips over hers and pulling away. But she wouldn't let him. She closed the space between their bodies, pressing her lips to his, and he instantly tightened his grip around her.

The moment was incendiary. The kiss deep and passionate. His apartment was silent, but they could both hear the thunder of their heartbeats. The air between them was almost crackling with electricity.

And then they were moving.

He pushed her against the wall of glass, pressing his body to hers, entwining his tongue with hers. Setting her aflame. His hand left her waist and travelled up her arm to cradle her face. She kissed him as if he was all the air she needed. He felt her hands run down his body and she tore his shirt out of his trousers, plunging her hands under it, feeling his skin and the ripples of muscle.

His low groan at her touch surprised them both and he slowed his lips. Then pulled away.

The ferocity of what he felt surprised him. Alex had had many conquests in his life, but this was the first that had affected him so strongly from the first touch. He needed to create just a little space.

'I offered you a drink,' he said slowly, still holding her in place.

He couldn't seem to let go. The way the light caught her eyes and made them sparkle was arresting. He reached up and pulled the silver pins from her hair, sending locks of brunette hair tumbling around her shoulders. She was breathtaking.

She smiled coquettishly. 'I don't mind skipping that.'

* * *

Emma wondered who this person was wearing her skin tonight. She wasn't normally this brazen. She was a quiet, usually shy copywriter. But this new side of herself made her feel alive.

Alex chuckled and planted a quick kiss on her lips, but before she could respond he was walking away. 'What can I get you?' he asked as he pulled off his bowtie and tossed it on to one of the large couches.

'Surprise me.' She took a seat at the kitchen counter, watching him prepare their drinks. 'You're good. Ever been a barman?'

He laughed openly. 'No such luck. I've just learned how to make things I like.'

'Does that mean you can cook?' Emma watched him pour an amber drink into two crystal glasses filled with ice.

'Yes, but nothing terribly fancy.' He handed a glass to her before taking a sip from his own. 'Now, I think I promised you a view.'

He laced his fingers in hers, pulling her into an indoor elevator that ascended to a private rooftop terrace. If Emma had been captivated by the view from the inside, it was nothing compared to being up here. The Melbourne skyline sat twinkling behind her while the sea stretched before her.

'Wow,' she breathed. 'If I had this, I would never be inside. How are you not out here all the time?' Her eyes didn't leave the darkened horizon.

'Because I don't work where I play,' he replied easily.

She eyed the pool, casting a blue glow over the space,

and somehow understood. 'You're all about rules, aren't you?' she asked.

'They keep life simple.'

Emma couldn't disagree with that. She took a sip of her drink. It was sweet and minty, and utterly delicious. 'I would never have had you pegged as a Stinger man.'

'You want to know a secret?' he asked.

She nodded her head.

'I prefer whisky, but it's always useful to try to impress a beautiful woman.'

Emma laughed. She didn't think he would need any tricks. He was perfectly capable of being impressive all by himself. 'I don't think you need to try very hard. That accent is sexy enough.'

'Is it?' A smile played on his lips.

'You know it is.'

It was turning out to be a much better night than she could have imagined. She felt so much lighter away from the masquerade. And even though she stood there drinking a delicious drink, still admiring an amazing view, nothing could take away the awareness of her body to Alex's proximity.

As if he had a direct line to her thoughts, he suggested they retreat indoors. He invited her to get comfortable on the large plush couch that was devoid of his tie. The crystal glass in his hand was tipped back, and he was draining the last of his drink and placing it on the glass coffee table with a clink. Then he undid the button at his throat and joined Emma on the couch.

He pulled the glass from her hand, setting it down on the table in front of them. Anticipation thrummed through her body. He slid his hand into her hair and pressed his lips against hers, then pulled away, then did it again. Light, teasing kisses were placed on her lips and jaw and neck, and when she tried to pull him back to her lips he was already there. Soft lips roving over hers. His tongue was teasing, seeking permission, and her lips parted for him. Emma could still taste the minty sweetness of his drink on him.

His kisses were a heady thing, and she could feel heat pooling in her centre. He was being so gentle, but then he slanted his head and it built the kiss to a whole new connection. Deep, passionate, consuming. And she was falling. Her fingers were grabbing fistfuls of his hair. Nails scraping against his scalp.

Alex moaned against her lips. He pressed his body against hers, pushing her down into the couch cushions. His hand slid along her body and hitched her leg up. He was pressing his hardness against her sex, making her moan out his name. His kisses became hungrier. Fervent. Her breath was already coming in short pants, and they were still fully clothed.

'Tell me what you want, Emma,' Alex said as he trailed hard, lustful kisses down her neck.

'You. All of you. More…' she panted.

His hand travelled over her shoulder, down her side, where he found the zip of her dress and slowly, maddeningly, pulled it down. Swathes of blue satin parted. A shiver trembled through her as his warm hand ran over her bare skin. He kissed her shoulder as he pulled the strap of her dress down and she wanted to be free

of the constricting thing. All she wanted was to feel
Alex's lips on every inch of her.

Sensing her need, he reared up, sliding the dress off
her, uncovering her body and dropping it to the floor
in a pool of fabric.

Emma watched him unbuckle her silver stilettos.
First one, then the other. Both shoes hit the hardwood
floor with a clatter. And then he was kissing her again.
Moving his mouth up her leg, his nose brushing over
her covered sex, lips caressing her belly, her breasts,
before finally his hand slipped under her and unclasped
her bra. A giggle escaped her as he tossed it over his
shoulder, not caring where it landed.

His mouth closed over her nipple, and she drew in a
harsh breath. It was as if a taut line tugged at her centre, and she knew he was only going to build her tension up more. Drive her mad until his name was all she
could say all night.

Long, skilled fingers played with the band of her
panties before dipping under, running through her slickness, and he groaned. Before she even registered what
was happening, her panties were off and on the floor
and Alex's mouth was on hers, demanding and desperate. No one had ever kissed Emma as he did. As if she
was all that existed. As if she had been made to drive
him wild. But drive him wild she did.

Alex reached out and picked an ice cube from the
glass that sat on the coffee table. 'Open,' he instructed
gruffly, bringing it to her lips.

She obeyed without hesitation, sucking the cold
block. Her gasp broke the silence as he took back the

cube, leaving a cold, wet path in its wake as he trailed it from her lips and down her chest and around her nipples, which hardened instantly. Goosebumps erupted over her skin. A shudder passed through her.

And then he was moving the cube lower and lower, until she squealed as it touched the apex of her thighs. But his hot mouth was instantly on her neck, and the sensation between hot and cold was setting every nerve-ending alight.

Alex's mouth continued its sensual assault on her senses, and he was about to drop the cube on the table when she pulled his hand to her mouth, wrapping her lips around the now substantially smaller block.

His eyes were intense and then his mouth was on hers. Tongues entwined until he pulled the cube into his own mouth with a grin. Her laugh rang out. Emma had wanted fun and now here it was, dressed up as the devastatingly handsome Alexander Hastings.

She kissed him with abandon. Her tongue searching his mouth for the hidden ice cube. She took it back, but not for long. Alex showed her the ice cube, held between his teeth. There was a twinkle in his eye as he crushed it. Loudly. Telling her that he had had enough of being teased.

He settled himself at the foot of the large couch, taking her hips in his hands.

'Alexander…' she breathed, watching his head dip down. Feeling his cold mouth on her sex.

As her pants and moans filled the air, as her chest rose and fell with the sweet torture of Alex's tongue, it seemed he was enjoying this. That it pleasured him to pleasure her. This man was so completely different from anyone who had come before. Emma had always been a little shy, but by no means was she a prude. She enjoyed sex just as much as the next person, but in her short and somewhat sporadic dating history no one had ever set her world alight like this.

*Careful,* a voice within her warned. *This is just fun. One night. He's a playboy and you don't do relationships.*

Emma shut the voice down and gave herself over to the explosive sensations that were making it hard to breathe. Higher and higher she flew. Her peak was in sight. He held her tight, watching her run her fingers through her hair as she came apart.

He stretched along the back of the couch, pulling Emma into his arms. Holding her until she was able to catch her breath.

'Shall we take this to the bedroom?' he asked, brushing her hair away from her face.

'Yes.' She nodded.

He scooped her up into his arms and marched, barefoot, down the passage to his room. A big, plush, warm space that overlooked the sea on one side and the city on the other.

On any other night it would have been a view to marvel at, but now the only view she craved was Alex above her, and below her, and losing control because of her.

He sat her at the foot of his bed and gave her a quick, hard kiss.

'This is hardly fair,' she complained. 'You're still clothed.'

'Then do something about it,' he whispered into her

ear, making something in her belly unfurl. How was he able to do that to her with just his voice?

The thought occurred to her simply to rip his shirt apart, but it was probably very expensive, and she would feel guilty, so instead she slowly unbuttoned the shirt from the bottom up, hoping she would drive him as insane as he did her.

The shirt parted, revealing his impossibly toned body. He really must live by rules, because that body would not be a possibility without discipline. Control.

She kissed his taut, rippling belly and moved to push his shirt off his shoulders, but he held his arm out with a smile tugging at the corner of his lips. First one cuff was undone, then the other. Then the white shirt fluttered to the floor and Emma's hands were already pulling off his trousers. Tugging off his boxer briefs, which he kicked aside. Emma hadn't even noticed when he'd lost his socks and shoes.

Alex was magnificent. Everything about him was perfect. From his chest, to his voice, to his kisses, to his impressive hardness.

Emma wanted to taste him. Kiss him everywhere. With a wicked gleam in her eye, she licked all of him. The groan he let out was deep, almost animalistic. Spurred on by his reaction, she gripped his length, passing her hands over it a few times before taking him in her mouth.

'Emma…'

It was a strangled sound that ignited her blood. She twirled her tongue around his tip, teasing him. His strain and pleasure could be seen on his face and tensed muscles. What was happening to her? She was never this playful in bed. She felt…unleashed.

'Emma, I'd like to make love to you.' His voice was hoarse, gravelly. 'This feels too good.'

She wanted that too, so she let him pull away from her. Allowed him to press her down onto the pillows before he reached over and pulled a foil packet from the bedside drawer.

Her eyes were drawn to his shoulder blade. The very proper, very handsome Alex had a tattoo. She drew herself up behind him, her fingers going to the amazing ink work. It was a globe. A map of the world held in a gyroscope. The contrast of the black ink on his light skin was stunning.

She placed a kiss on it. 'This is beautiful.'

Alex kissed her sweetly. 'You're beautiful.'

He tore at the foil pouch and rolled the latex on. The moment he did Emma was there, pushing him down on his back. Straddling him. She lowered herself on to him with exquisite slowness, heard his breath released in a hiss.

Something about the way Alex looked at her made her feel brazen. In control. Even though he was making her world spin off its axis tonight. He let *her* lead. Let her use *him* for her pleasure. It was exhilarating.

Being with Alex made her realise just how lacklustre her previous experiences had been. It wasn't as if he was blowing her mind into orbit. No. Every touch, every groan, the feeling of him being inside her, his eyes never leaving hers, the fact that he never once bothered hiding his pleasure was pinning Emma to the moment. Forcing her to absorb every drop of pleasure.

But when the rhythm of her hips faltered, he rolled her onto her back and took back control.

Alex had always had more than his fair share of female attention. He'd never really had to try very hard, and he'd never seen the point of doing so. It was just a physical release, and every one of those women had understood that it would be for only a night, even if they wanted more. He liked it that way. *He* never wanted more, never missed them when they left.

But now there was Emma. And suddenly he couldn't imagine feeling this for only one night. She was a drug, and he'd been hooked from that first kiss.

His hips sank deeply into her. Ecstasy flowed through his veins with every thrust. He couldn't remember sex ever feeling this good.

'You're so damned amazing,' he breathed into her ear, and felt goosebumps erupt on her skin.

He kissed her long and slow, until he felt a coiling at the base of his spine, the tension in every corner of his body, like a guitar string pulled tight. Alex could feel Emma was near her peak. Clenching around him. Holding on. Climbing towards her *jouissance*.

'Emma…' he groaned.

He heard his voice come out breathless and tight, and it seemed to push her over the edge. Her head was thrown back in rapture as she came apart, and then he did too, growling into her neck. His release was violent, explosive. Unlike anything he'd felt before.

When his senses returned, Alex felt delicate lips kissing his shoulder. Soft hands caressing his back. And he wanted more.

He eased out, settling alongside her and wrapping an arm around her shoulders, pulling her close. Pressing a kiss to her hair.

'That was incredible,' she said.

'I'm not so sure,' Alex teased. 'We might need to try it again.'

She playfully smacked his chest and he caught her wrist, running his thumb over the simple black outline of a cat that was there.

'Didn't think you were the only one with a tattoo, did you?' she said.

'Why a cat?' he asked.

'Because it's Lucky,' she said, and then, seeing the look of confusion on his face, continued. 'Lucky is my cat. I got this when I rescued him. He's actually my first pet. Though I think I'm his most of the time.' Emma laughed. 'What about you?'

'I've never had a pet,' Alex stated blandly.

'Never?'

'No. There's a couple of Airedale Terriers at the family manor, but I hardly ever go back there.'

Alex caught himself before he said any more. He didn't understand why he was volunteering information about things he would never talk about usually. Things he liked to keep buried. Things that hurt to think about.

'But that's enough about that,' he said with a smirk, before rolling over her and silencing her with a kiss.

# CHAPTER FOUR

EMMA AWOKE WITH the sun streaming in through the glass wall. The rays warmed her back as she lay ensconced in the soft sheets of a large bed. It took her a moment to register that she wasn't at home, and she bolted upright. Then the night came flooding back to her, and she couldn't help squeezing her thighs at the memory.

Of all the beautiful women at the ball, Alex had picked her. Her. She could still scarcely believe it.

Then she looked at the empty space beside her.

Alex was already up. Running her hands over the cool sheets, she thought he must have been for a while. And it was time to face reality. It had been one night, and that night was done. Alex had had his fun and so had she. Now she had to go back to being plain old Emma. Alone in her bubble—just the way she liked it.

Emma clambered out of bed and looked around for her clothes, then remembered that they'd littered the living room floor. Mercifully, Alex's shirt, discarded the night before, still lay on the carpet. Emma buttoned it up as she made her way to the en suite bathroom to freshen up as best she could before what could potentially be an embarrassing ride home.

Alex was tinkering around at the kitchen counter when Emma walked in. The entire space had been transformed. In the day, his apartment was bright and airy. It seemed as if the sun danced off every surface. He felt his mouth dry. Blood rushing south so fast his head swam.

Seeing her in his shirt made him want to take her back to bed. This woman had a power over him that he didn't quite understand. Attraction and lust were familiar concepts to him. But what he felt with Emma was on an entirely different plane. It had made no sense to him last night and it still didn't. Seeing her now, in the light of day in his apartment, and knowing that she would leave soon, made an ache grow in the depths of him.

He wanted more of her. No. He *needed* more.

Alex had always considered his home his sanctuary. Whether it was London or Melbourne. He never invited women there, choosing instead to take them to hotels or opting to go home with them. That was a reminder of how temporary their dalliance was. He had all the power over when he would leave, and there would be no reminder of them afterwards.

He was very aware that he'd broken that rule last night. Even more confusing was the fact that it didn't bother him in the slightest.

'I made you coffee,' Alex said, handing a mug to her.

'Thank you.' Emma relished the aroma before taking a small sip. 'Where's yours?'

'Right here,' he said, holding up a teacup.

She couldn't help the chuckle that escaped her, but it didn't seem to bother him. He pinned his blue gaze on her as he drank, and she was putty all over again.

*What the hell, Emma? Get it together!* she mentally chastised herself.

To give herself somewhere else to look, she located all her missing garments.

'You know, I actually come down to the beach here every weekend,' she said as she picked her shoes off the floor.

'You do?'

'Yeah, I like taking a walk in the morning and then getting a coffee.' Emma ran her fingers through her hair, hoping to smooth it out into something presentable.

'I might have to join you the next time you do that.'

'You're welcome to.'

Her phone buzzed on the marble countertop. There were a few texts from Hannah, making sure Emma was still alive and berating her for not texting back. Emma quickly responded with an apology, telling her best friend that she was fine and asking after her cat. Lucky would be fine, if a little angry with her.

Her phone beeped in her hand. The message that came through immediately got her hackles up.

'Breakfast?' Alex offered.

He made it sound like something sinful, but Emma was still scowling at her phone. It was a text from Lauren, summoning her to their parents' too large home in Toorak. It was by no means a difficulty for her to go…

it was just a lot further than she was willing to go after such a spectacular night.

Picturing Lauren's face in her mind, not to mention her father's, she knew she would be walking into a berating because Alex had chosen her. It didn't matter what lies Lauren had told her father—the actual reason for her fury was that. Lauren believed that she deserved every special thing. Good things weren't meant for Emma.

Lauren's hatred of Emma had started early. She was older and had become used to being favoured. That was until they had started school. Quiet and studious, Emma had impressed every one of her teachers. Something Lauren had not done. Emma had continued to impress everyone as they'd grown older. And so the put-downs had begun, and had followed her right into the family business where Lauren would not have Emma upstaging her in front of outsiders.

She was the eldest. She was meant to take over from their father. Unfortunately Emma was still expected to give her all to the company. It was her duty as a Brown to ensure that the company prospered even if she would never be given a fair chance there.

But today Emma was riding a wave of absolute bliss and she was just not ready to crash. And that was exactly what would happen if she left.

She closed her eyes and took a deep breath. She felt calmer when she opened them. And then she thought, why shouldn't she spend a little more time with Alex? Last night had been an eye-opening experience. The sex had been unreal...

* * *

Alex was watching her with curiosity. He should have been trying to get her out through the door, but if he was honest with himself he really wasn't trying to get rid of Emma at all. If anything, he was picturing her laid out on all the various surfaces in his penthouse.

'You know what, Alexander? I'd love breakfast.'

His smile stole her breath, and she knew she'd made the right choice.

He took her clothes from her hand and dropped them to the floor. Her shoes clattered loudly in the silent space. Was it really silent? Because Alex clearly remembered switching on music, just as he did every morning. But he didn't hear it now. Emma was biting her lip, and that was all he could focus on.

'I really like the way you look in my shirt, but I think I like it off you more.'

Then his fingers were deftly undoing the buttons, pushing it off her shoulders. He brushed his mouth over the smooth skin and heard her breath hitch. The shirt fluttered to the floor and he lifted her up, placing her on the marble countertop. A gasp left her lips as her warm skin made contact with the cool surface, but his lips and hands were already on her, to chase the chill away and make her burn.

He ran his tongue along her lips and felt her shiver. Deepening the kiss, he pushed her down against the marble. Alex wanted to take his time with her. Enjoy this while it lasted. Because in a few short hours she would be gone from his life.

Except he couldn't take his time.

Laid out on the marble top, she made him hunger in a primal way. He feasted on her, making her writhe and pant until she was a mass of quivering need.

'So beautiful,' he said gruffly against her skin.

His praise made Emma feel as if she was flying. It was easy to see why he was never short on female company. She was just another conquest in a life full of them. The thought burned like acid. Would she be forgettable to him? Emma wanted fun. No strings. But she also wanted someone to think that she was special.

Emma pushed the thoughts away, focussing on how good he made her feel. His mouth closed over her breast and she didn't have to try very hard. Her fingers sank into his soft dark hair, holding him in place. His tongue was sending bolts of pure pleasure right to her core. Alex covered her hands with his, pulling them away and pinning them against the counter before his lips sought hers once more.

'Alexander, please…' she whimpered. Whose voice was that? It certainly wasn't hers.

'Please what?' he taunted.

She tried to press her body to his in any way she could.

His dark, teasing chuckle reached her ears and the sound of ripping foil brought her back. She realised that he no longer had her hands pinned down. She tried to push herself up on her elbows, but he put a hand on her shoulder to keep her down and slowly pushed into her. Her eyes fluttered closed and he stopped.

'Eyes on me,' Alex said breathlessly.

His blue eyes were so much darker. His pupils blown out. Emma felt the breath leave her. Then he began moving his hips.

His hand was moving up to her neck, his thumb caressing her lips. Emma pulled his thumb into her mouth, sucking it. Twirling her tongue around the digit. Making him groan her name. It was beyond erotic to watch what he was doing to her as he was setting her world alight.

She could feel herself drawing closer to the precipice. And then she was exploding around him, taking them both over the edge.

They needed more than just a few moments to catch their breaths.

'Screw breakfast,' Alex said, once they had.

She laughed as he led her back to his room. Being with him was drugging, and she just couldn't have enough of him.

# CHAPTER FIVE

IT WAS QUITE a while before either of them was ready to surface for sustenance. But eventually, shirtless, with his trousers hanging off his hips in the most delicious way, Alex led the way to the kitchen.

Unfortunately, the fridge was mostly bare.

'Sorry, my housekeeper hasn't been in yet.' He closed the fridge door and turned around, drawing Emma into his arms. 'How about I take you up on your promise to show me around Melbourne?'

Emma wasn't sure she wanted to traipse around the city in her clothes from the ball. But she definitely didn't want to take Alex home with her, where Hannah would be waiting with a million questions. This was just a moment of pleasure. She should leave. The problem was that having his hands on her drove an insatiable hunger for him. And a bit of air would be good. Some space for them to collect themselves.

'I'd love to, but I can't exactly wear what I have here to go sightseeing.'

'That's easily fixed.' Alex pulled his phone out of his

back pocket and after a series of rapid-fire taps slipped it back in. 'All taken care of.'

'Alexander...' she scolded.

'Emma...'

The way he said her name was a caress. Like silk over her skin.

'If you keep looking at me like that,' he said, 'I'm going to have to keep you here and we'll both starve.'

His words made her want to combust. The fact that she was affecting him like this made her feel seen in a way she hadn't ever been before. But, as much as she wanted to spend the day in his bed, she hadn't eaten anything at the ball and was well and truly ravenous.

'Why don't you go and take a shower and we'll get going soon?' he said.

'Okay.'

Emma stepped under the spray in Alex's ultra-large bathroom, a little disappointed that he hadn't chosen to join her. She could think of so many things he might do with the shower head that was hooked on the wall...

She shook her head. When had she become this person? Emma didn't date much. Her parents' marriage was more than enough of a warning against the entire institution, and when she had once found someone she genuinely liked he had chosen Lauren over her. Of course he was old news to both of them now. But the pain of that still stung. No one had ever chosen her over Lauren. Not until last night, that was.

Alex made her feel renewed. And if that made her a little greedy for his particular brand of sex, then she was all for it. She wasn't looking for love, and it was obvious that neither was he.

Emma turned the water off and pulled two fluffy towels off the rack, wrapping her hair in one and the other around her body. She padded out to the lounge, where she found him relaxing on the couch with his phone in his hand, looking far better than anyone had the right to in a pair of dark wash jeans and a Henley shirt. His aviator sunglasses were hanging off the neck of his top. His hair was still damp.

She would never understand how men were able to be ready in a few short minutes.

He looked up from his phone and his expression went from one of concentration to one of pure hunger. It made her squirm where she stood.

Then Alex picked up the bag beside him and walked over to her, dropping the handles into her hand. He smelled like shampoo and something woodsy. Spicy...

'Thank you,' she said. Her voice barely came out at all. She cleared her throat and tried again. 'I'll just get changed.'

She dashed back into his room, finding jeans, a shirt and sneakers in the bag. She dressed quickly and brushed out her damp hair in the bathroom, then rushed out so she wouldn't keep him waiting any longer.

'I don't know how you managed to get my size right.' She laughed.

His smile was wicked. 'I undressed you, remember?'

Her face burned. How could she forget?

'Shall we?'

She nodded and walked with him out of his apartment. When they entered the lift she stood away from him. His proximity was a danger to her libido. She saw his smile and knew that she was being glaringly obvious.

'This way,' he said, walking towards a pearlescent white Porsche SUV.

It looked faster than it had any right to, being so large. From the lip over the rear windscreen to the low tyres, with bright red peeking through black-spoked wheels, the whole thing screamed speed.

'So you're an SUV person?' Emma observed.

'I'm nothing if not practical.'

'Practical?' She laughed. 'Is that another rule? It can be big as long as it's fast?'

His grin was infectious. 'Almost right. It can be mine as long as it's fast.'

Emma barked out a laugh and it felt great. Being around Alex made her feel lighter. It also made it harder for her to breathe. Especially when he smiled like that and it lit up his face. Like the sun coming out on a cloudy day.

Alex, charming her with his chivalrous manners, opened the door for her—something no one had ever done for her before, not even her father. Although he would always show that courtesy to Lauren and Maddison.

She didn't know why it surprised her coming from Alex. Maybe it was because he had the air of a caged animal just waiting to be set free.

He eased the car out of the parking structure and onto the road. Emma kept shooting covert looks at him. His long fingers were gripping the steering wheel loosely. Those shades were hiding the eyes that had made her come apart this morning. Being in a car with him felt like being trapped in a stifling heat that she both wanted to escape and never leave.

He seemed so in control. He *always* seemed in control. Even when he let her take the lead in the bedroom. But Emma didn't mind, because his competence felt really damned good.

He looked over at her and a slow smile spread across his face. The air in the car became suddenly thicker. As if he could tell exactly how affected she was, his smile grew into a grin.

But before she knew it they were parked, and he had come round to her door holding it open for her.

'I thought Fed Square would be a good start,' he said.

Emma's fingers twitched towards him. She shoved them in the pockets of her jeans to stop herself reaching out. 'I agree.'

It was a place she had come to often. After a long day battling her family, it felt great just to be a nameless face in the crowd, sipping a cocktail while the sun disappeared behind the tall buildings.

She doubted today would be nearly as relaxing. Having Alex walking beside her, she felt hyper-aware of his presence. Of the space between them and how easy it would be to close it. But she couldn't. She didn't even know what she was doing here. Her night of fun had turned into a morning of fun, but at some point they would have to bid each other farewell and go their separate ways.

That was what should happen. But, heaven help her, that was not what she wanted.

Alex let her lead the way to a restaurant she liked. They were soon shown to a table and he sat down opposite her.

'So, what are we having?' he asked, picking up the menu.

Emma had no idea. She was struggling to have the words make any sense at all. When the waiter arrived, she randomly picked something and hoped it would at least taste good.

Looking for something to fill the silence in the waiter's absence, Emma spoke of all the attractions the city had to offer. It sounded like rambling to her own ears, though Alex seemed to be getting caught up in her passion for this city.

She was overjoyed when her phone beeped with a new message.

What do you think you're doing?! You were supposed to be here hours ago!

Lauren. The smile was wiped off Emma's face immediately. Hastily she shoved the phone into her back pocket and found Alex's intense blue gaze on hers. She plastered a bright smile on her face, but he wasn't fooled.

'Just my sister,' she said dismissively.

Alex had been cursing himself for suggesting they come out at all, because all he wanted was to be buried in Emma again—and that was a problem. He'd never had an issue sending a woman on her way after a night to-gether. Yet he was craving Emma like a drug.

And right now he was still curious about the reaction she'd had to her sister at the ball, and again to her message that morning. He felt curiosity and another feeling he realised was a protective instinct. He'd noticed how her shoulders had sagged just a fraction when she'd read that text, and he wanted to put himself between her and whoever wanted to hurt her. Shield this beautiful, passionate woman.

It was an alien feeling that he pushed away with great difficulty, focussing on the curiosity. But Alex wouldn't ask her about it. As a rule, he never involved himself in the lives of the women he slept with. Never helped with their careers—even if he could. There was a solid line between business and pleasure. And an even thicker one between any kind of pleasure and actual feelings. He would not give them the wrong idea, and the last thing he needed was a relationship.

But what he did want was to enjoy Emma a little more, and if he was going to see this attraction out he needed to know more about her.

Being who he was, Alex was careful. 'So tell me, Emma, what do you do at Brown Hughs?' he asked.

Emma's momentary shock was covered by a small laugh. Of course he knew where she worked. He was rich and powerful. There was probably an entire background check on her already compiled.

'I'm a copywriter.' She said the words stiffly.

'Doesn't sound like you enjoy it.'

He was far too observant for Emma's liking.

'I feel like I can do so much more than I am, but my dad says I'm needed in copywriting so that's where I'll be. He's the boss.'

Unfortunately for Emma, having her father at the head of the table had not helped further her career, as it had for Lauren or Maddison. She could still hear his words, spoken so long ago. *Everyone tells me you're intelligent, but I just don't see it.*

Emma forced the memory away, not wanting it to spoil what was a pretty mind-blowing morning.

'If you want more, Emma, then take it,' Alex said.

'Spoken like a master of the universe. Is that what you're doing in Melbourne? Taking more?'

*And running from ghosts.*

He shut the thought down instantly.

He was done with London.

He wasn't going to think of his mother. Not now.

'Yes. Hastings International has a very long history. It started after the war, to rebuild, but in all those years its potential has never been maximised. No growth further than Europe.'

'And that's what you want to do? Grow it?' Emma asked.

'Yes. I want to see it on every continent.'

She smiled. 'Something tells me you'll do it.'

'Without doubt.'

Alex winked. His passion was contagious, Emma thought. Everything about him seemed so deliberate.

So intense. It was as if he blotted out everyone else because he was the sun, and Emma ached to burn.

Alex leaned forward. 'Tell me...' he said. 'Why do your sister's texts get under your skin?'

Emma had hoped that she was being at least a little successful at hiding her irritation. Clearly she wasn't. She debated how she should answer. There was no way she was going to tell him how much she envied the love and attention Lauren received. Nor would she tell him how much Lauren detested her. In the end she settled for an edited truth.

'We have a bit of a love-hate relationship,' Emma said lightly. 'My mother should have dealt with it—I'm sure you know what that's like.'

She was certain that Lauren wouldn't have listened to her mother, though, and once she'd involved her father, her mother would have backed down anyway.

'Not really. I don't have a mother,' he replied.

Emma's cheeks flamed red. 'Oh! I'm sorry! I didn't mean to be insensitive.'

Alex seemed to realise what he'd just shared and brushed it off. 'Don't worry about it—really.'

Their meals were served and the awkward moment was quickly forgotten. Especially when Alex noticed a little drop of cream at the corner of her mouth. He wiped it off with his finger and she felt her heart stutter as he licked it clean. She could feel the burn in her cheeks.

'Was that good?' she asked, somewhat breathily.

'Yes,' he said. And then he leaned closer and whispered, 'But you taste better.'

A shudder passed through her. They needed to leave before they were arrested for public indecency.

Once they were finished Alex paid, despite Emma's protests. He knew there was still something he needed to make clear.

'Emma, I need to be honest with you. I don't do relationships. I do simple, and fun, and then it's over.'

He held his breath, waiting for an embarrassing explosion that never came. Alex firmly believed that love was for fools. It simply didn't exist. Lust was real. Tangible. Something that was irrefutable and then, once indulged, gone. A fleeting thing that made sense.

'That's good, because neither do I. I like simple. Simple is good,' she replied.

'In that case, Miss Brown, lead the way.'

They left the restaurant and Alex noticed Emma sliding her hands into her pockets again. He wanted to yank them out and place them around him. Wanted to wrap his arm around her as their feet swallowed up the ground underneath them.

He couldn't do that. She was affecting his sensibility. But that wasn't the person he was, and he wouldn't give her any hope that he could be. So he widened the gap between their bodies.

And immediately regretted it.

This was actual torment. He tried to seem laid-back, but felt his body pulled taut like a bowstring.

They went to watch the yachts and boats on the Yarra— or at least tried to. They stood so close together that he

could feel Emma's heat. His arms ached to slide around
her as they leaned on a concrete balustrade. But he
couldn't touch her after what he'd just said to her. Not
out here. Not when that would make it seem as if they
were some sort of couple.

Emma couldn't know that his hands were clasped so
firmly together so that he wouldn't be tempted to kiss
her in front of all of Melbourne. Tempted to make her
moan out his name with the city before them, making
it theirs. He pushed off the rail. They had to keep moving. He had to get himself under control.

Alex pushed his sunglasses high up on the bridge
of his nose, taking a last look at the river. It was a reminder of all the loves he'd found and indulged by himself. Alone. He was better off that way.

Emma took them on a walk through Alexandra Gardens and past the Arts Centre, but as they made their
way back towards the city he was barely paying attention to where they were. All he could feel was Emma's
presence, and all he wanted was to be back in his apartment, where his hands could be all over her.

He could bear it no more.

'Emma,' he said, pinning her against the wall in a
spectacularly graffitied alley, where the walls were an
ever-changing work of art. 'I have to tell you I really
don't care about seeing the city. I just want to get you
back in my bed.'

He could barely believe that he wanted to take her
back home. Sending her on her way was the smarter
plan. But how smart was it to deny himself? Emma

knew the score. This wasn't about feelings or a relationship. It was just sex.

'Give me the weekend,' he said. 'I promise you won't
regret it.'

He heard his voice, low and rough. He could see in
her eyes that she knew just how aroused he was. And,
with his body against hers, that she could feel it.

'I want that too,' she breathed.

'What I said before still stands. This doesn't change
things.'

'I know that.' She grinned. 'I don't want it to.'

His lips crashed down on hers. The moment they
were on her it was as if he was breathing again. Living
again. Flying again. His hands were underneath her
shirt, sliding under the waistband of her jeans. Squeezing her butt.

'These things have been driving me nuts all day,' he
growled in her ear. And she laughed.

Voices grew closer and reluctantly Alex pulled away
from her, not sure if that kiss had taken the edge off or
made him thirst for her even more.

# CHAPTER SIX

THEY BARELY MADE it into his apartment before their hands were all over each other and they were leaving a trail of shed clothes to his couch. Afterwards, they lay together, catching their breath and enjoying the feeling of being close.

In an unguarded moment, Alex wondered why such a vibrant woman didn't want a relationship. In his experience all women did. Even the ones who knew they would never get it from him but still hoped they might be the one to change his mind. His mind couldn't be changed. He had seen what the illusion of love could do to a person, and he had no intention of turning into his father.

With Emma it was different. But what could have happened to her for her to be as cynical as him?

The feeling of gentle fingers tracing patterns on his chest put an end to his thoughts. It felt as if her touch left a trail of fire on his skin.

Alex lifted her fingers to his lips, pressing a kiss to the soft pads. He opened his eyes and found her gaze on him. His heart stuttered. Her lips were rosy and full from his fevered kisses. The scent of his body still lingered on her skin. It surprised him how much he liked that. To have marked her as his to enjoy. The possessiveness alarmed him.

Alex pulled away to try to break the spell—only he couldn't leave. The electricity between them hauled him back.

Emma's fingers threaded through his hair, tugging him towards her. She kissed him, trapping his lip between her teeth. Giving him a little nip that walked the fine line between pleasure and pain.

'Witch,' he growled, and she laughed with wicked delight.

The ringing of his phone pierced through the moment, vibrating loudly on the glass table. Alex ignored it, sliding his tongue over hers. The phone wouldn't stop.

'You should get that,' said Emma.

'They can call back.' His voice was like gravel.

Still the phone kept going, until he picked it up with a frustrated sigh. He pressed the button on the side, silencing the device even as he registered the name on the screen. Feeling a niggle of guilt, he tossed it back onto the table, trying to remember a time when he had ever ignored his father's call.

Alex loved and admired his father, but Robert Hastings could hardly complain about being ignored. Not after the way Alex had grown up.

He dropped a steel shutter on those thoughts. He wasn't going there now. Not when he had a beautiful woman in his arms.

'Now, where were we…?'

* * *

Emma could see that the playful twinkle in his eye had been replaced by a harder look. A haunted one. She wanted to ask about it, but then it occurred to her that it really wasn't any of her business. Asking about his feelings wasn't keeping things simple. She doubted he would tell her anyway. Still, she wanted to make it better somehow, and there was one way she knew she could.

'Somewhere around here…' Her lips found his once more.

The sun had gone down and the bedcovers were carelessly tossed over Emma's bare back. Alex sat against the headboard, an arm draped over a raised knee, gazing down at her porcelain skin. Wanting to kiss every freckle.

*What are you doing, Hastings?* he asked himself.

He wanted to have another day with her tomorrow. And it didn't seem as if it would be enough.

Alex swung his legs off the bed, too much on edge to get any sleep. Work was always a welcome distraction. Pulling on his jeans and shrugging his shirt back on, he picked his phone off the nightstand and quietly left his room.

After pouring a measure of whisky into a glass, he replaced the stopper on the crystal decanter, setting it back on the bar, and stood by the large window overlooking the sea.

The shrill cry of his phone punctured the silence.

He answered quickly, and the screen filled with his father's face.

'Dad.' Alex placed his glass down on the coffee table and eased himself onto the couch upon which, a few short hours before, he'd had Emma panting his name.

He shoved the image aside.

'Alex. How are you, son?' asked his father.

Judging by the dark wood bookshelves behind him, it looked as if he was in his study at the family manor Alex so rarely visited.

'I'm well. Looks like you've taken a trip.'

'A bit of country air does you a world of good.'

'So you always say.' Alex smiled.

'I do.' Robert chuckled. 'Besides, there was a soirée…' he rolled his eyes at the word '…that I just did not have the patience for. A bit of peace and quiet is what I need.'

Alex knew what that meant. His mother Catherine would have been there. That was the only reason his father would miss a society event that would have undoubtedly required his presence.

*'We are the Hastings family. We have obligations we cannot turn our backs on,'* he had said to Alex when he was growing up.

His mother was the only reason his father would have ignored such a commitment. But Robert would never want to speak of it, so neither would Alex.

'I know why you called,' he said. 'I've been looking through the reports. My projections for the Australian expansion are on track.'

'That's what I like to hear.'

Alex and his father had always had a cordial relationship, if a somewhat stiff one. It was just the two of them. A team. Even though as a child he'd sometimes felt like the benched teammate. That hadn't stopped him from growing into his power. He knew where his father's boundaries lay, and Robert trusted his son immensely. So much so that when Robert had stepped down, there was no question of who would take his place with the family legacy.

Even though he didn't need to, Alex liked keeping his father included in the running of Hastings International. It was a company that dealt with major construction, engineering and architecture amongst other things. A company meant to build, not tear down. He could tell Robert appreciated it, and discussing business felt good.

It was a bit of normality after being trapped in a lust-filled haze. And yet even though this was what he lived for, Alex wanted nothing more than to end the call, march back into his bedroom, strip the covers from Emma and take her again. Alex was always in control. Never ruled by his hormones. He valued logic over emotion, and it was driving him insane that when it came to Emma he seemed to be a slave to his baser urges.

Alex was about to end the call, but his father stopped him. 'Before you go…are you okay, Alex?'

'Fine. Why?'

'I get the feeling you have something on your mind,' his father said.

Alex ran a hand through his hair. 'There's a risky proposition on the table. I'm debating the merits of pursuing it,' he said.

He had no intention of explaining that the proposition was Emma.

'Son, the bigger the risk, the bigger the reward.'

'Not always,' he said under his breath.

His father clearly knew he was talking about something else.

'No, not always,' he said. 'And that's why it's a risk. But you're a lot more careful than I was at your age, Alex. Trust your gut. You'll figure it out.'

Alex ended the call and tossed his phone onto the couch cushions. He swallowed his whisky in one, relishing the burn at the back of his throat. He had to figure this out—because he wasn't going to end up being an old man sitting in his study, hiding.

No one would get the better of him. He wouldn't allow it.

Dawn was breaking. It was Monday, and still they hadn't had enough of each other. With each kiss the spark didn't die. It didn't even fizzle. It just kept burning brighter. But the weekend was over and the sun was rising on the end of their tryst.

A delicate kiss on Emma's neck had a smile curving her lips. Alex rolled her onto her back and kissed her slowly, completely. His hand ran down her arm and disappeared under the dark sheets. Teasingly, lightly, he moved it over the smooth skin of her belly and over her sex. She arched into the touch. Her fingers fisted in his hair as she moaned into his mouth.

His hands were such sweet torment. Pulling her apart and piecing her together. With her eyes closed and his lips everywhere, and the promise of blissful rapture dangling in front of her, Emma could barely breathe. She couldn't remember where she was. She didn't even remember her name. All she knew right now was Alex. His touch. His smell. His strong arms that felt far too safe for her sanity. She was trying to hold on to all of it. Every sensation. Commit it all to memory.

'Emma,' he whispered in her ear, 'let go.'

And she did. Shattering with a muffled sob.

His lips came to hers, kissing her until she came back to him. 'Hey...'

He smiled with that megawatt beam. It made her stomach flutter. With an intense look in his blue eyes, he brushed her hair away from her face.

Emma felt like the person she wanted to be when she was with him. Bold and strong. Feelings she often had to keep tethered. But she didn't need to with Alex. There were no expectations. No risk of her disappointing him because that wasn't what this was about.

This was a break from reality. From everything she was expected to be and couldn't live up to. But now it was over. So she would go back to being alone and having no one but Hannah and her cat.

'Emma,' Alex said evenly. 'I want more than a weekend. Nothing has changed. I just want more of you.'

That screamed danger to Emma. More time with Alex was beyond appealing. She hadn't ever experienced this chemistry with anyone on her short list of previous lovers. Looking back, it felt as if all those affairs were in black and white and now she was seeing in splendid Technicolor.

'Alexander...'

'Please.'

'I want more too,' she said, abandoning all good sense.

Why shouldn't she have a bit of fun? Emma always did the right thing. What was expected of her. What everyone else wanted. Well, now she wanted Alex, and the world would just have to continue without her because she was due some happiness.

The words had barely left her lips when Alex swooped down, claiming her. Branding her. His tongue slid over hers, dominating her. It wasn't a gentle kiss. It was a kiss of possession. Of pure want and desperate need. He swallowed Emma's moan and then had to tear his lips away from hers, smirking at her mewl of protest.

Alex kept his intent blue gaze fixed on Emma's as he brought his phone to his ear. She could only just make out a woman's voice on the other end.

'Reschedule my meetings,' he said, without a greeting.

Emma squirmed as his eyes darkened, pinning her in place.

'I don't care. The board can wait. Something's come up.' He ended the call and placed his phone down.

With limbs that felt like lead, Emma fired a text off to the only person she needed to—her manager, Greg. Emma was a Brown, and for once she was going to take advantage of the liberties her name brought her. To hell with what anyone thought. She was living for herself right now and it was liberating.

Her phone slipped through her fingers onto the bed-ding as Alex's fingers slid into her hair, tilting her face up to meet his.

'You're all mine.'

The words set her on fire.

# CHAPTER SEVEN

EMMA WOKE TO find herself alone in bed. After Alex had shown her exactly how pleased he was that she'd agreed to spend a little more time with him, loose-limbed and fabulously exhausted, she had dozed off.

She could hear the shower running. Surprising Alex under the jets was too tempting to resist. She threw off the covers, but her phone buzzed against the bedside table. Emma had no intention of answering it, but then she caught the name on the screen. It was Maddison.

Where are you? Dad's fuming.

Emma didn't know why. There were no urgent meetings that required her to be there. Nothing at all going on that would make her father notice her presence. Or rather absence. He barely acknowledged her existence anyway. Everyone was well aware that, despite how hard Emma had worked earning her degrees, and the hours she put in at the office, she wasn't the daughter he intended for the C Suite. All his talk of her 'duty' was just to make sure she would do what he needed her to without question and would stay out of his hair. Because no matter what Emma did, her father would always make her feel like a burden.

Emma wasn't going to respond, but she saw the three little dots that told her Maddie was typing another message.

Actually, don't tell me where you are. Can't say anything if I don't know. Can't believe you ditched! Video call in ten. There's an announcement.

Emma groaned. There had been talk all week of this 'announcement', but no one in her family seemed to want to make it. Until now. Dread settled like lead in her belly.

Emma scooped up her clothes off the floor, quickly changing into her jeans and rushing out of the bedroom. Slipping into the other bathroom, she made sure she looked presentable before taking a seat at Alex's large dining table, which seated twelve. It was a quiet space that they hadn't once used. Idly she wondered if he had it there just to fill what would otherwise have been an empty space. But thoughts of Alex's social life were wiped from her mind the moment her phone began to ring.

Whatever they were going to say, Emma was determined not to react. Fixing in place the mask of indifference she often wore at work, she answered the call.

Her father sat at the head of his meeting table, with his business partner to his right and her mother to his left. Maddison sat beside her, with Lauren opposite and the head of HR taking the final occupied seat.

'Good day, everyone,' Emma greeted.

Anxiety bloomed in her chest. She could handle herself at work without batting an eyelid. It was what she'd spent so many years studying for. To prepare herself to one day lead the company in some way. The problem was that no matter how hard she tried to separate the two, her family life was inextricably woven in with her work life. She would never be able to escape that, and now, looking at her father, she felt her confidence waver.

'Emma,' her father said.

Peter Brown was a large man with greying temples and dark hair. He had cunning hazel eyes that, despite their colour, held little warmth. They simmered with anger now. A look she had often seen directed at her mother during their blazing rows. But the one thing his treatment of Emma had done was make her strong. So now she could hold her phone in her hand and appear to all that she was unaffected by him.

'We have an announcement to make, and we need you to stand beside your sisters tomorrow when we do.'

'Okay…' Emma said hesitantly, unsure of what was coming. She just knew she wouldn't like it.

Alex shut off the taps and left the en suite bathroom. He smiled inwardly at the disappointment of finding the bed empty. Shaking his head, he opened the closet door to get out a set of clean clothes. That was when he heard Emma's voice, and another. She was on a call, by the sounds of it. Nothing unusual about that, except something made his skin prickle.

Dressing quickly, he followed the sound of her voice

to find her at the dining table. A little vertical line had formed on her forehead between her furrowed brows as she listened attentively, not noticing his presence in the doorway.

Alex knew he should be giving her a bit of privacy. After all, he never appreciated being eavesdropped on. But something about the way she sat, so stiffly, and the way her voice tried to show no emotion at all kept him in that doorway. Watching.

'We have taken the decision to move Lauren up to be VP of Services…'

Emma clenched her jaw as her father spoke, remaining silent.

'…and Maddison will be taking her place.'

'So Maddison is now my boss's boss?'

Emma hadn't meant for the words to sound as sharp as they had. Especially when Maddison shot her an apologetic look. But it hurt. Again. Her younger sister, less qualified and less experienced, was now soaring far higher than her in the career stakes.

Part of her was happy that Maddison was getting some recognition for the work she'd put in, but the biggest part of her saw this for what it was. Evidence that her sisters would always be chosen over her, no matter what she did to prove herself to her father.

'Yes. Can we count on you to do your duty to this family?'

Hearing her father ask the question crushed her. After everything she had done, she'd hoped her commitment to her family, to the company, would never be in question. Seemed she was wrong.

'Of course. I will always do what the company needs me to. Tell me what to do and I'll do it,' Emma said. 'I just have one question. How did the vote go?'

'It was unanimous, darling,' her mother said.

*Unanimous.* She should have expected it. 'I see.'

Emma managed to keep her voice steady as she tried to quell the crushing disappointment that was ripping at her insides. That one word meant that even her mother, whom Emma had always been close to, had chosen Maddison.

It was no real surprise, if Emma was truly honest with herself. Internally, she was glad that for once she'd decided to do something that made her happy. Any tiny trace of the guilt she'd felt when she'd agreed to spend more time with Alex vanished.

'That's it. Your mother can give you the details.'

Her father was already closing his leather folder. Emma knew when she was being dismissed. She took no notice of the two people who were not her family as she bade them a cordial goodbye. At the table, though, her nails were leaving crescent-shaped marks in her palms. The pain of her clenched fists helped her keep the mask of professionalism in place.

As soon as the call was over, the mask slipped completely. She dropped the phone to the tabletop and ran her fingers through her hair. Closing her eyes, she willed herself to feel calmer.

It didn't last a moment.

Her phone rang almost immediately. It was her mother.

Emma hit the red button. She absolutely did not want to speak to her. Not when she had listened to Emma's frustrations, told her to hang in there, that her time was coming. Lies.

It rang again. This time it was Maddison. Her call met the same fate. Emma wasn't upset at Maddison. The only thing she was guilty of was being just a little spoilt, but she was the youngest. It was to be expected. And Emma was guilty of doting on her too. She just couldn't bear to speak to any of her family.

*Why should I be upset?* she asked herself.

She had known this was coming. That there would be a time when Lauren and Maddison would flourish from their parents' favour and she would languish in a little corner of the company where her father would never have to be bothered by her.

She couldn't leave either. Peter and Helen Brown both expected their daughters to work in the company. Leaving would be the ultimate slap in the face to her parents. There was still an expectation of her that she could never be free of.

'Emma?'

Her head snapped up at the sound of Alex's voice. 'Alexander... I hope you don't mind... I needed a quiet place to take a call.'

He strode towards her, taking a seat at the large table. His eyes were unreadable. 'What's wrong?'

'Nothing.' She forced a brittle smile.

'Emma,' he pushed. 'Talk to me.'

She looked into his eyes. They were intense. Unre-

lenting. And suddenly she wanted to tell him everything. Tell him about all the ways her family had hurt
her. This was just sex, after all. She could say anything
to him. Because at the end they were just going to walk
away. Every secret would be safe because it would mean
nothing to a stranger.

Emma closed her eyes and took a deep breath, feeling more in control when she opened them.

'It's just that I thought if I proved myself, studied
hard and worked my way up, I could *be* someone in
the company. I never once expected just to walk into a
management job. I was prepared to work hard for it. But
the same doesn't apply to my sisters. Lauren was pretty
much gifted her position, and Maddison now has been
too. Do you know how humiliating it is to constantly
get passed over for promotion after promotion in your
own father's company? I'm stuck as a copywriter because apparently that's where I'm needed and I should
do it out of duty.'

'Duty' was just a nice word for the expectations
forced upon all three of the Brown daughters. Lauren
and Maddison relished their roles. Emma was alone in
her feeling of being trapped. She had one shining light
in her life with her charity work, but even that was
frowned upon by her father. Money always came first.

'Duty doesn't fulfil you,' Alex said.

'No, it doesn't. But what choice do I have? I am
who I am.'

Emma thought about the massive house her parents owned and the tiny flat that she'd bought and

now shared with Hannah. She thought about the luxury cars her family had and the sporty little hatchback she owned. Who was she really? Yes, she was a Brown, but she had been trying to distance her life from her family for a long time. To escape the hate and the vitriol.

'Anyway, it doesn't matter. I knew it would come to this.'

'Why?'

Emma roughly pushed out her chair and stood by the window. With her back to him, she could hide the tortured expression on her face. Only Hannah truly knew what growing up had been like for her.

When she spoke her voice was even. Emotionless. She saw Alex frown. 'Because Lauren was always preferred over me. In every way. My father adores her. I tried to prove myself to him, but the only people I impressed were the ones who would never have any say in my life. Maybe I remind him too much of my mother. God knows, he hates her.'

She gazed out into the distance. The sea was so tranquil. Focussing on that made talking easier. She felt Alex move behind her, but he didn't touch her. He was waiting for her to finish what she had to say.

'My parents had Maddison to fix the cracks in their marriage. They were more like gaping chasms.' She laughed without mirth. 'My father was opposed to the idea initially, but when Maddie almost died during the birth, it changed his attitude. He'd almost lost her.' She finally turned around and looked into those intense blue eyes. 'So, you see, I can't compete with that. I'm not going to get a fair chance.'

'You don't have to deal with any of it. Leave. Do what makes you happy.'

'It's not that simple,' Emma said quietly.

Alex shook his head and took her face in his hands. 'Everything is simple. Life is a choice, Emma. People choose how to treat you. You choose whether or not to accept that. You can't make people stay if they have chosen to leave. You're worth more than that.'

Why did he have to be so kind? Why did this man, whom she had known for such a short time, have to treat her with so much care? Make her feel seen? Say all the words she wanted to hear? Why did they have to come from the most temporary person in her life?

Emma looked away from his intense gaze. He was making her feel things, and that wasn't what she wanted. Especially not now, when she felt vulnerable.

When she let her eyes meet his again he lowered his lips towards hers, hovering above them, waiting for a sign to say she wanted this too. She closed the gap between them, ignoring any warning that his kiss might mean something more. She didn't need or want that. All she wanted was the distraction.

Alex pulled her against his body as he stepped backwards, reaching behind him for a chair that he dragged out. His lips left hers as he sat down. His eyes, though, were unwavering in their steely focus on her. She straddled his lap and his arm locked around her, the other brushing her hair back. He took her lip between his, gliding his tongue along it, and her breath left her in a sigh.

This was what she needed. To be so consumed that she had no room to think about anything else.

# CHAPTER EIGHT

ALEX COULDN'T STOP thinking about what Emma had said. Every instinct had screamed at him not to get involved. Not to ask her what was wrong. But seeing her so deflated made something flare within him. A protective instinct he hadn't felt before for anyone other than his family and his company.

And that kiss afterwards. Another mistake. He was fully aware that he was breaking his own rules. The funny thing was that he couldn't bring himself to regret it. He'd wanted to kiss her and he wasn't going to deny himself any part of Emma. That was why he'd asked her for more time. Once their time was up there would be no reason to see any more of each other, so he was going to savour every kiss and touch he could with her.

That was why he had arranged this evening. Emma had had a trying day that he had done his best to make her forget. Now he was taking her out to dinner so that they could have a good time. It would be a good memory for her and it meant nothing more than that. He was convinced of it.

The dress that was laid out on his bed was there so

that she would have something to wear, not to make her feel special.

Alex took a sip of the whisky in his hand, watching the lowering sun.

Emma stood by the bed, her fingers caressing the diaphanous fabric of the pale green dress. All Alex had told her was that they were going out for dinner tonight. By the looks of the garment on the bed she could only assume it was somewhere special. Apart from their brief adventure in the city, it would be the first time they were leaving the apartment in days.

The thought made her blush.

A small smile played on her lips. Whatever Alex had planned would be fun, and after all that had happened she needed it.

Not knowing what the next day would bring, Emma was determined to enjoy tonight. She picked the dress up and stood by the long mirror, gliding the smooth, silken fabric over her body. Fastening the straps behind her neck, Emma examined her appearance.

It was a beautiful dress, falling like a waterfall to the floor. It made her feel sexy and powerful and so very feminine. She buckled her strappy heels in place and was ready to go.

The breath was knocked out of her when she stepped into the lounge.

Alex slowly pivoted from the window, his searing gaze devouring her whole. In a suit several shades darker than his eyes, he looked like a builder of empires—or someone who could just as easily tear them down.

He extended a hand to her, and as if instinct alone drove her Emma crossed the room to take it. He pinned her hands behind her back, making her thrust her breasts out, her body pressed against his. Light as a feather, his lips trailed down her neck.

'Right now, I want to say screw dinner…but the car is waiting downstairs.'

His gravelly words had electricity firing in her core. He kissed her hard and quick, a promise for later, and with a warm hand on the small of her back led her out of his apartment.

The driver waited beside a black limo, opening the door the moment Alex and Emma appeared through the glass door.

'Pulling out all the stops, aren't you?' Emma laughed.

Alex simply shrugged with that smile she adored. He helped her in, then settled beside her, pulling her against his side with an arm wrapped around her.

The last time they had shared a back seat he'd wanted his hands all over her. It took a monumental effort to look away from her, so that he could control the temptation. Now it was different. Emma had agreed to be with him until they'd both had their fill of each other, which meant he could touch her to his heart's content.

'Where are we going?' Emma asked as the limo pulled away from the kerb.

'To dinner,' he said with that secret smile, and he pressed a button that had the privacy screen shut firmly in place.

'Yes, Alexander, but where?'

'You're not very patient, are you?' He draped her legs over his lap and whispered in her ear. 'Maybe I just need to occupy your mind with something else.'

He slipped his hand under her dress.

'Alexander...'

'Emma,' he mimicked.

His hand slid up her smooth leg, caressing her sex, pushing her lace panties aside as his fingers found her core, making her gasp loudly.

'You have to be quiet, Emma,' he whispered in her ear.

She was trying, she really was, but it was impossible with his fingers sliding into her. So he covered her mouth with his and swallowed her every gasp and moan as he thrust his fingers back and forth. Simultaneously pulling her apart and making her soar. And when she reached that pinnacle and shattered, she plummeted back down in a million pieces. But gravity wasn't pulling her to the ground, it was to Alex instead. His arms and his lips and his warmth. And when she finally opened her eyes, his were right there, ready to receive her.

'Welcome back,' he said with a wolfish grin. He righted her dress and pressed a kiss to her temple. 'We're here.'

Emma looked out of the window. They were in front of one of the tallest buildings in Melbourne. The setting sun was glinting off the mammoth glass and steel structure. Slowly, she moved her legs off Alex. They still felt a little shaky from his expert touch, but she didn't have time to recover.

The door was being held open, and he unfolded himself from the car with enviable grace and held out a hand to help her. Her face burned as he held her close, keeping her steady on her feet as they walked towards the entrance. Except she noticed that Alex wasn't leading her to the restaurant, but to a bright door next to it.

'But it's closed today,' she said with a frown.

'Not to me.'

Was there nothing beyond his reach? she wondered. Emma had enjoyed a very privileged upbringing, but at no point had she got to enjoy this kind of power. All Alex had to do was snap his fingers and he sent the world spinning in whichever way he wanted.

They walked through glass doors framed by bright yellow panels that bore the word 'Skydeck'. There was only one person waiting in the dimly lit foyer, who greeted them and pointed them in the direction of the elevator that would take them to the viewing platform.

Alex hit the button for the eighty-eighth floor, and almost instantly Emma felt the whoosh as the lift rocketed up through the floors. Her ears were popping a little as they ascended.

'Have you been here before?' he asked. She saw there was something like uncertainty in his eyes.

'I actually haven't. Feels like something you should experience with someone, and Hannah is terrified of heights.'

'So, a first?' Alex said.

The thought was mirrored in Emma's mind, but she shut it down. There was a first time for everything. That didn't have to make it some sort of revelation.

Faster than she had ever experienced, the lift came to a halt and the doors slid open.

'Shall we?'

Alex held out his arm and Emma linked hers through his as they stepped out into a wood-panelled passage that opened out to a wall of glass that beckoned her. Melbourne lay sprawling beneath her feet. The setting sun to her right cast everything as far as the eye could see in bright gold. And she could see so far.

She could see the ferry at the pier that seemed so massive from Alex's apartment. The mountains in the very distance. And the Yarra snaking through the city. Parts of it glistening like sequins, other parts in dark shadow. It was beautiful.

She had almost forgotten that Alex was standing beside her. She gave a slight start when he spoke in her ear.

'There's more to see.'

Of course there was. Her face split into a grin as she looked past him to a lit sign that said 'Edge'. It took more self-control than she had known she possessed to walk elegantly up a roped-off ramp. Another attendant waited there. After a warm welcome, he slid the door open on an entirely black antechamber.

Emma was buzzing with anticipation. This was something she had always wanted to do and now, thanks to Alex, the experience was hers. There wasn't another soul around. There was no rush. It was all theirs.

She stepped into an opaque glass cube, her heels clicking on the fine surface.

'Enjoy.' The attendant smiled before closing the door.

Emma stood at the rail as the cube began to move

forward. She felt Alex stand behind her, his arms coming around her, caging her as he placed his hands beside hers on the silver rail.

'How long do we have?' she asked.

'As long as you want.'

It felt as if he was offering her the world on a platter. The inherent danger of the feeling was lost to her excitement. The cube had stopped moving. She stopped breathing. All at once the glass went clear, and everything was lit with the last rays of golden sunshine.

'Alexander...' she breathed. It was breathtaking. She wanted to take it all in at once, but there was so much to see.

'You wanted a view.'

And he had given it to her. Then she looked down through the glass floor and swayed. It was a daunting thing to look hundreds of metres straight down to the city below.

His arms wrapped tighter around her. 'I've got you.'

Emma leaned into his embrace, her eyes never once leaving the view. And that was how they stood, bodies pressed together, with nothing needing to be said as the sun sank below the horizon.

As the sky became inky, more and more lights began to twinkle below them. Suddenly the barely discernible streets became snaking paths of gold. The steel and glass structures around them weren't glowing but glittering, as a sea of lights reflected on their surfaces. Everywhere she looked, it was as if a new sequin came to life.

From up here everything seemed so small. Inconsequential. Her job, her family—none of it mattered. They were all just a blip in the tapestry of this city. Well, almost all of them.

Emma hazarded a glance behind her and saw Alex's gaze fixed on the distance. She had called him a master of the universe, and he had never looked more like it than right now. The world was his to do with as he pleased.

'Thank you, Alexander.'

In that moment, standing high above the dazzling city she loved so much, she felt every bit of the hurt and disappointment of earlier fade away as if it had never existed. All there was, was her and Alex and this amazing sight. A gift that only he could give her.

Turning in his arms, she held the lapels of his jacket, raised herself up and kissed him. He kissed her back. Claiming her just as much as she was claiming him. With all the fierceness she had in her…alight with passion and daring. Bold as she could be when she didn't have to hide.

Her fingers moved up to his dark hair, tangling in the soft strands as his hand travelled up to her neck. He kissed her deeper, making her burn before he broke the connection of their lips.

'Are you ready to go back?'

She took one last look behind her and nodded. Alex kept his eyes on her as he twirled his finger in the air and the cube began to slide back inside the building. When they walked back in, there was an attendant holding a tray with two glasses of champagne. Alex handed one to her, took the other in his hand.

She drew up to the large window with him beside her. 'This was perfect.'

She clinked her glass against his and took a sip of the cool bubbly, her eyes catching his, and she knew that he was reminded of the very first drink they'd shared, just as she was.

# CHAPTER NINE

EMMA HAD BEEN to her fair share of fancy dinners. Every manner of restaurant openings and A-list events. It came with the territory. Brown Hughs was a large, well-respected PR and marketing company, and Emma's surname meant she was inevitably taken along for the ride. But even though she'd had all those experiences, none of them compared to sitting across the table from Alex, with the city far, far below them, admiring it through the floor-to-ceiling windows next to her with not another soul in the restaurant.

Somehow Alex had managed to book the entire place. An award-winning kitchen was at work just for them.

They didn't even bother with menus. They were enjoying a seven-course dinner of the chef's finest food.

Alex sat back in his chair as the server cleared away their empty plates. His eyes were intense in the dimly lit restaurant. Light and shadow engaged in a battle over his sculpted face, making him look even more predatory than usual. Emma was fighting the urge to crawl over the table onto his lap, and almost as if he could read her mind he smiled at her.

A cheeseboard and the most artistic dessert Emma had ever seen were placed before them. Before she could even thank their server she was gone. Still, Alex didn't take his eyes off her.

Emma shook herself free of the spell he had placed her under. Despite what their relationship was meant to be, she wanted to know so much more about him. What he had done for her tonight was something she would treasure always. But there was still so little she knew of him, and it didn't feel right to scour the internet for answers now that she knew him. She had a feeling that what she found wouldn't accurately reflect the man in any case. Every time he avoided saying something she would see the shutters falling in his eyes, and it made her want to know more.

'So tell me…in this arrangement of ours, am I permitted to get to know you better?' she asked.

Alex chuckled. 'What do you want to know?'

His eyes followed the movement of her lifting her spoon to her mouth, closing her lips around the silver, and for just a moment it looked as if his pupils had blown wide, and his throat bobbed.

'You mentioned that you don't often go to your family manor. Why is that?' Emma asked.

Alex kept silent. The heated look in his eyes cooled. She could see a muscle flicker in his jaw.

'Alexander? Am I not allowed to know the answer to that question?' she asked lightly, trying to keep the atmosphere between them upbeat.

He was quiet for so long that Emma thought he wouldn't answer at all.

'I've never really liked the manor. It's been in the family for generations. The first son and heir gets it, along with the title. That's how it became my grandfather's, then my father's, and one day—'

'Yours.'

'Yes.' Alex crossed his arms over his chest.

'But you don't like the place?'

'I don't like the expectation.'

Alex looked at her and she could see the pain he tried to cover up behind his eyes.

'It's beautiful enough—if a bit old and boring.' He chuckled. 'But once it's yours you're expected to be the master of the household—ensure you have an heir.'

'Be Earl Hastings.'

'Yes, and that pressure can make you make mistakes. Trust the wrong people. I would rather just be Alexander Hastings, brilliant CEO, than Earl in a place I barely visit. It's just another thing I don't need handed to me.'

Alex kept his eyes on hers, but his voice was more subdued than Emma had ever heard it.

'Is that why you said duty doesn't fulfil you?' Emma asked.

Alex didn't reply.

She fell silent, pondering his words, and placed her silverware down. 'Do you think that people think you've had everything handed to you?'

'I know they do, Emma.'

'Is that why you work so hard? Why you want to turn Hastings International worldwide?'

'Partly. It's not just because I have something to prove—it's also because I see potential that's never been exploited. I see the company for what it could be, not just what it is.'

'Alexander, I don't think anyone could accuse you of being entitled. You have nothing to prove.'

'If only that were true,' he said softly.

Emma wanted to reach out to him. To touch him. But the faraway look in his eyes made her hold back. There seemed to be so much weight on his shoulders. A weight that was a different kind of duty from what she had to bear. She understood that. Still, there was much he'd revealed without saying much at all. The one thing that really stuck with her was his comment about trusting the wrong people. It made her wonder if he had trusted someone he shouldn't have, or maybe his father had.

She wanted to ask about it, but he jumped in before she could utter a word.

'My turn.' He unfolded his arms and leaned forward, placing a perfectly cut piece of cheese on a cracker that he held to her lips. She crunched into it, and he took the remaining piece into his own mouth. 'I understand why you might not like your sister. I don't understand why she would dislike you.'

'All Lauren's ever known is being preferred over everyone else. That's her spot in the world and she likes it. On the few occasions when I had something she didn't, or received praise when she didn't, it irked her. It wasn't the natural order of things. It got worse at school, because I had a natural inclination towards academia and she didn't.'

Emma shrugged.

'I guess as we got older the prizes we competed for were greater, and she thought they should all be hers. I don't know why she bothers, to be honest. I'll never be a threat to her. If anything, today was proof of that.' Emma picked up her spoon again, twirling the silverware between her fingers. 'I asked how the vote went and my mother said it was unanimous, so I know I wasn't even considered. Not by anyone.'

That was what really hurt. Emma was well aware of how her mother felt about Maddison. She tended her more closely than anyone else, and Emma understood why. Nearly losing her had left a scar on Helen's soul, which was why she would always coddle her youngest daughter. But Emma had hoped that for once emotion wouldn't rule. That her work and dedication would speak for itself.

'Doesn't surprise me, though. You get used to knowing your place in the world.' Emma looked down at her food, concentrating extremely hard on the culinary art on her plate. Or rather, trying very hard to ignore the stinging in her eyes. 'I wanted to be close to Lauren for the longest time, but we only ever got close to that dynamic when I kept well away from all that was hers.'

Alex nodded. 'If you could leave, what would you do?' he asked, taking a sip of his wine.

'I help to run a small literacy charity. The work is amazing, Alexander!'

She smiled as she explained about the classes that were held a few times a week, where she taught people how to read. About all the colourful personalities she got to meet from different countries and impoverished neighbourhoods.

'I try to give as many weekends and afternoons as I can. We have a little team that carries most of the load. I do what I can.'

'Is that what you would like to do?'

'More than anything! Just doing it a few evenings doesn't feel like enough, but I can't get time off work to give more. As it is, my father hates it that I do it. "A waste of time" is what he calls it.'

Emma would never forget coming home from university and telling her parents that she'd decided to volunteer. Her father had told her that she'd proved that she wasn't one of them. That if she could waste time with schemes that made no money, then she had plenty of time to dedicate to the company. Money came before all else to Peter Brown, and Emma knew that would never change.

'Then do it, Emma,' Alex said.

'I can't, Alexander.'

'Why not?'

'Because I'm a Brown. There are expectations. I can't just go off on the charity path—it doesn't work like that.'

'Emma, life is too short to just do what's expected of you.'

Emma shrugged. 'Do you have any siblings?'

Alex huffed a laugh. 'No, the closest thing I have to a brother is Matt, a friend of mine. It was just my father and I until I went to boarding school, and he was always busy.'

'That sounds lonely…' Emma thought that at least she'd had Maddison, and sometimes even her mother. She was suddenly struck by the image of a lost blue-eyed boy and her heart broke.

With a wave of his hand, Alex brushed the image aside. 'It's no easy thing for my father, being who he is.'

There was admiration in his words. Emma wondered what it must be like to admire one's father. As awful as she felt every time she thought it, she couldn't see a single decent thing about hers. And she knew why.

*'I never wanted you. You were just a mistake your mother refused to fix.'*

Just a few words, callously tossed her way, had had her believing she was unworthy of love. But love didn't exist, so what did it matter?

A warm hand taking hers had her returning to the present. To the piece of pure perfection who was looking at her with so much warmth and heat that she wanted to lean into him. Because, as she was quickly realising, Alex was her favourite distraction from all things real and painful.

'Would you like to go?' he asked.

'I think we should.'

In barely any time at all they were back in the limousine and the door was shut. Emma didn't even notice that, and nor did she notice Alex holding her firmly against his side. A scene at the entrance to the residential tower was captivating her. A father was holding the hands of both his daughters, then he stopped and knelt to tie one of the girl's shoelaces. He gave her a little hug and the other little girl jumped onto his back. Smiling broadly, all three of them disappeared into the building.

She was still staring after them when the car began to move. How she had craved that kind of affection growing up, and never once received it. Watching that little family, she thought it seemed like such an easy thing to do. Be happy. Maybe it was. Maybe the problem was her. After all, it was only her that her father couldn't love.

Whatever it was, Emma was done with dwelling on it for now. She had just had the most amazing evening in a very long time after all.

Alex nuzzled Emma's neck, coaxing her back to him.

'Where have you gone?' he whispered in her ear.

'Nowhere I need to be.'

She turned around and kissed him with a savage intensity that had him rueing how quickly they were approaching his apartment. Not that it mattered. Even as the car slowed he didn't let her pull away. The only break in their connection came when the door was opened and he led her into the elevator. And then his lips were on hers once more.

When the doors dinged open, he scooped her into his arms and somehow managed to get them back into his penthouse. He only set her down once they stood in the middle of his apartment, taking her face in his hands.

'I don't know where you went to just now, Emma, but that's not where you belong.'

He had noticed the desolate look on her face and he

didn't care to see it again. Not when there was so much life and passion in her.

A warning bell sounded in him, saying that he was starting to care for her more than he should, but he ignored it—because only a monster would not be moved by that expression. And, no matter what else Alex knew himself to be, cruel wasn't one of them. He knew cruelty, and he wouldn't wish it upon anyone.

Emma kissed him then. Soft and sweet and entirely soul-consuming.

# CHAPTER TEN

IT SHOULD HAVE been concerning that he couldn't keep his hands off Emma. That every time he had her it never satiated his thirst for her. But now, having her back pressed against him, his lips on her nape, concern was the last thing on his mind.

It had angered him to see her hurt. He wanted to bring a smile back to her face. Needed to. He tried to convince himself that it was just because she was upset. Because he could see how lonely she had been and that was something he knew well.

The truth that he didn't want to face was that her happiness made his cold heart beat with joy.

He wanted to make Emma burn for him. For her to feel. To forget the thoughts that she wouldn't share with him.

They were done with talking. It was a pointless exercise when in a few days Emma and him would be done and she would move on. He felt a flare of bright hot rage at the thought of Emma with someone else. It caught him off guard and he almost shook his head at himself. Of course Emma would move on—however she chose to. It wasn't any of his business.

'Close your eyes.' His breath caressed her skin. He could already hear her breathing deepen.

Having his low voice so close, his warm hands on her bare shoulders, not being able to see anything, was making heat pool in her belly. Emma couldn't think because, as if he'd flipped a switch, Alex had sensation firing over every part of her.

He eased the zipper of her dress down, moving his hand to unclasp the straps around her neck. She felt the rush of cool air on her naked skin as the dress fell to her feet, exposing her breasts and the flimsy lacy scrap that covered her most intimate parts. He let out an appreciative sound at the sight of her. Then his hands were stroking her arms and her shoulders.

'Alexander...' she moaned.

Teeth nipped at her ear. 'Say it again,' he commanded. And she did.

Emma could feel the effect that she had on him through the fabric of his fine suit trousers, pressed against her back.

Alex guided her arms around his neck, making her thrust her chest out. 'Keep them there.'

Another instruction in that seductive accent.

Emma swallowed thickly. With her eyes closed and her arms raised behind her she was completely at his mercy. Yet it only made her feel alive. Every scrape of his stubble against her skin, the touch of his fingers as they glided down her arms, trailing over her stomach, made her feel electrified. As if she was buzzing with a current that came straight from him.

She shivered as his hands slid under the scrap of lace, guiding it over her hips, sliding it down her legs. And then one jacket-covered arm wrapped around her waist, holding her firmly, brushing against her already fevered skin. His other hand travelled down to her sex, and she let out a cry somewhere between a moan and a mewl.

He had to hold her tighter, because she was sure her legs would buckle if he didn't. And when he sucked on the juncture between her neck and her shoulder all she could do was feel. Feel him everywhere as she reached for her shattering climax, letting go completely in his arms as her breath hitched, then halted, then came in shuddering pants.

'Emma…' he whispered in her ear, but she couldn't form words to respond just yet, and she felt his chuckle reverberate through her.

Alex kept holding her, until she was finally able to turn around in his arms. He had a wild look burning in his blue eyes, and she shivered again because it felt as if a wolf had been unleashed upon her.

'I want to touch you,' she said.

Wordlessly, Alex stepped away from her, shrugging off his jacket and dropping it to the floor in a rumpled heap. His intent gaze fixed upon her, he went about divesting himself of his clothes. Every movement of his body was controlled.

He held out his arms—an invitation for her to touch him as much as she wanted.

Heels clicking on the wooden floor, Emma stepped

out of her shed garments and into his embrace, running her hands over the contours of smooth muscle up to his neck and then standing on tiptoes to kiss him. Her hands didn't stop wandering until they tangled in his hair.

'More…' he breathed against her lips.

*More.* It was a simple word that did more than any praise ever could. It made her feel awakened. Emma was holding the key to his pleasure. She was powerful, and the realisation of that made her smile. Grin. Until a bubble of laughter broke out of her.

Alex had never had an issue with touch. It meant very little. People touched him all the time. The women he slept with, the people he worked with… But nothing had ever felt quite like Emma's touch. As if his skin was being branded. As if she was lighting a flame from the inside. It calmed his heart and had it racing all at once.

He pulled back to see a bright glint in her eyes. He could see her strength reflected in them. Despite everything she had against her. No. Not despite. *Because* of everything she had against her, she was stronger than anyone he knew. Stronger than even she realised.

This was Emma in all her glory.

He wanted to drop to his knees and worship at her feet, but that wasn't who he was. Alex didn't do softness, or all those other things that made one weak. He didn't do love. Was incapable of it. But what he could do was allow her to take a little control and feed the fire that he could see in her now.

He retrieved a foil packet from his wallet and tore it with his teeth, but Emma took it from him. Throwing his head back, Alex groaned as Emma rolled the protection onto his hard length.

'You're always prepared,' Emma teased.

'Being around you, I have to be. You're a siren, Emma.'

Using the tenuous hold he had on his control, he poured himself onto the couch, feet planted on the floor, back straight. He crooked his finger at her, beckoning her to come closer, and when she did he pulled her astride his lap and folded his arms behind his head.

'You wanted to touch…so touch.'

It was a challenge. He knew Emma recognised it for what it was. A gift. One that would let her exert her will in the way they'd both enjoy best.

She trapped her lip between her teeth, looking down at him as if he were a treat. A meal to be devoured. Maybe he was—but so was she. Alex curled his hands into fists. He felt his nails scraping against his scalp, and that helped him keep still when all he wanted to do was sink into her.

Emma felt slightly daunted. After all, there probably wasn't much that Alex hadn't experienced. What could she do that would blow his mind the way he constantly did hers? Then it occurred to her that it didn't matter—because so far he had found pleasure in everything. So she did the first thing that crossed her mind. She kissed him. Hard. In a clash of teeth and tongue as her hands travelled down his body.

He made a strangled sound as she gripped his hardness, guiding it into her as she lowered herself onto him until there was nothing between them. It was the most arousing sound she had ever heard.

Emma started to grind her hips against him and felt his every muscle tense beneath her like cords of steel. Ripping her lips away from his, she leaned against him as her breaths came in short pants. Then she reached around him, taking his hands and placing them on her breasts, shattering his control catastrophically.

Alex's arms moved around her, holding her back as his mouth closed on one nipple then the other.

'I wondered how long you'd last…' She laughed, never having seen his blue eyes quite so dark before.

He growled. 'What are you doing to me?' And then he was kissing her again, pulling her body against his as they rocked together, barrelling towards their release.

Emma pulled away from his kiss, tossing her head back. His arms tightened as her squeal turned into a whimper, and he groaned a guttural sound as he followed her into the clutches of rapture.

She slowly opened her eyes to find that he held her against his chest. The safe weight of his arms on her back was telling her that he had her. They were both covered in sweat. Chests still heaving. Emma crushed her lips against his, pouring everything she felt into the connection. It was past tears, or pain, or happiness, or elation. She felt all of those things right now, but she also felt the shackles of them falling off her.

Alex couldn't understand why sex with Emma always felt so earth-shattering. And it was a dangerous thing, because how could he ever have enough? He had never grown dependent on anything—but this, with Emma, felt like an addiction. He knew right then that what he needed to do was get dressed and ask her to leave. Instead, he held her close, until her breathing evened out. She was so still that he wondered if she had fallen asleep. But she hadn't. She just couldn't bring herself to move away from him.

'I have to go to work tomorrow,' Emma said.

'And you're wondering how you're going to make it through the day without this?' Alex teased, even though he wasn't far off the mark. They had used up all of their time. It was back to the real world. 'Matt arrives tomorrow.'

'So it's just as well that I have to leave.'

'What are you talking about?' Alex shifted, forcing her to sit up and look at him.

'The weekend's over, Alexander. Today is over.'

'Emma, I said I wanted more of you. I didn't say it had to end tonight.'

'But if Matt arrives tomorrow, what does that mean?'

'It means that my friend will be in town and it might be nice to have a Melbournian to show us around. I do believe you offered your services as a tour guide.'

As he spoke, Alex could feel a prickle of unease telling him this was a bad idea. Flings weren't introduced to friends. This wasn't just breaking the rules. This was decimating them.

'I suppose I did.' She breathed out a chuckle. 'I just thought…'

'Emma, I want you here,' Alex said slowly. 'In fact, I'll be fetching Matt from the airport tomorrow and I'd

like it if you came over after work. Traffic is likely to
be heavy, so I'll give you a key to get in.'

'Really?'

'Yes.' He kissed her chastely on the lips. 'It's settled,'
he said, with an edge of finality in his voice.

The prospect of not having to end this for just a few
more days was too tempting to resist.

## CHAPTER ELEVEN

WHEN ALEX HAD said it was time for a drink, she'd thought he meant wine or coffee. Not the two bottles of water he was fetching from the fridge. Emma leaned against the counter on her elbows, admiring his sculpted muscular back and broad shoulders. He truly was the very embodiment of masculinity.

There had been a time when she would fantasise about someone like him. Unapologetic in his maleness. Strapping. Choosing her to love and be with. But that had been before her parents had eroded the very idea. Between their hateful bickering and her father's constant affairs, Emma had entirely given up on love. There was no such thing. And when she'd once thought she'd found someone to challenge that, just a little, Lauren had been right there to prove that Emma had it right the first time.

She hadn't given anyone her heart because there would never be a reason to. And now there was Alex, who believed the same. She had never had a connection to anyone as she did with him, and if even he believed that love was an imaginary construct, then it must be true.

Even if it wasn't, why would someone like him ever choose *her*? Emma had years of evidence that, given the choice, no one would choose her. If she thought about it, Alex had been careful to make sure there were barriers that weren't broken. In the overheard snippets of conversation on his phone and his driver in the limo, she'd heard them all call him Alex. Yet she didn't.

Emma didn't know why, but that thought stung.

'Alexander, can I ask you something?'

He turned around to look at her, sliding over the bottle of water. 'Of course.'

She wasn't looking at him. Instead, she ran her fingers along the patterns in the marble. 'Why do you let everyone call you Alex? Seems a bit familiar, given who you are.'

He placed his arms down on the counter, leaning in towards Emma. 'You mean why do I allow everyone to call me Alex but not you?'

He'd guessed her actual question. She didn't respond, trying not to show her hurt.

'Because, Emma, you're the only one who calls me Alexander.' He walked around the large island and pulled her to her feet, taking her face in his hands. 'And I love hearing the way you say it.'

'You do?'

He kissed her cheek.

'Mm-hmm. Especially when you're coming for me.' He kissed her neck. 'And when you think I'm being ridiculous.' He kissed her forehead. 'And when you're trying to get my attention.' He kissed her lips, slow and lingering. 'And when you want me to kiss you but you don't want to say it.'

He brushed his lips against hers once more and she was quivering with need all over again.

'But I'm really going to love hearing the way you say it when I show you your surprise.'

'A surprise?'

He nodded and pulled his trousers on, and draped his white shirt over her, fastening the buttons before placing a small kiss on her lips.

They went up the glass staircase and down a corridor she hadn't seen before. There were beautiful works of art lining the walls. From emotive photographs that captured a moment in breathtaking ways, to contemporary works in a myriad of colours. Emma looked at Alex, marvelling at the many sides of him and just how much of them he kept hidden.

'You ready?' he asked with a bright smile once they reached a closed door.

She nodded, her expression mirroring his. He held open the door and stood back to let her enter the cavernous room.

'Oh, Alexander!' she exclaimed on a breath.

It was a private library. There were shelves lining all the walls except for the one glass wall that during the day would bathe the room in light. Now, at night, it made the space feel cosier somehow.

Almost every shelf was filled to capacity with various books of different sizes and colours. Emma was drawn in. Stepping up to one of the bookshelves, she saw that some of the books looked extremely old. Probably first editions, she thought. She looked to her right and saw a ladder attached to a rail that would allow her to get a book from the very top shelf. She glanced behind her with barely contained excitement and saw Alex leaning against the back of a very comfortable-looking couch. There were so many places to sit. Lounge... Relax and forget reality.

'How—? You haven't even been in Melbourne all that long.'

Alex shrugged. 'I hope you didn't think that I'm just a pretty face.'

He pushed off the couch and moved to stand before her. Holding her shoulders, he spun her around and pressed his body against hers, making her step forward until she was right in front of the shelf. He held her hand in his and ran her fingers over several of the books' spines.

'While we're together,' he purred, his teeth grazing her ear, 'whenever you want a little escape, you can come here and take what you need.'

Her heart was thrumming, chest heaving. How could he affect her so deeply? She turned around and crushed her lips against his. He didn't falter for a second, catching her instantly and kissing her back.

Alex felt buoyant, seeing how happy the library had made her. How happy it made him. He had shared something of himself with her and Emma seemed grateful for the surprise, perhaps thinking it was his generosity that had led to him sharing it with her because books and reading were so close to her heart. But it was more than that. This room was his sanctuary too.

Alex pushed her against the bookshelf, kissing her deeply, but his phone chose this most inopportune time to ring.

'Dammit,' he growled, pulling the device out of his pocket. 'I have to take this—it's my father.'

Emma handed his shirt back to him and wrapped a throw around herself as he left the library, answering the video call as he went to his study. Calls from his father were usually about work. It was the easiest common ground to find between them as they built and rebuilt their relationship over the years.

'Hello, Dad.'

Robert Hastings took one look at his son and asked, 'Are you busy?'

'I have company,' Alex said simply.

Alex knew it wasn't his dishevelled appearance that had struck his father—rather the way he was looking. Somewhere between relaxed and annoyed at being disturbed. His father would have seen that look on his face a hundred times while he grew up. When he'd been completely focussed on something he enjoyed and had been disturbed. The thing was that even then he hadn't felt happy. Not like he did right now.

Alex wondered if his father had come to regret all the time he'd spent working. The time they had lost with Alex at boarding school, and then again when he had come home during the holidays and Robert had always been holed up in his study. It made Alex sometimes wonder how things would have been different if his father had been around more.

'How are you, son?' his father asked.

Alex frowned. 'Fine…' he said, feeling uncertain. 'I thought you were calling about work.'

'Can't a father enquire as to the state of his child?'

Alex laughed. 'Of course he can.'

'You have company, son. I don't want to interrupt. We can always talk tomorrow.'

'There's no need.' Alex jumped head-first into work and the two Hastings men talked business until they realised how late it had become.

When Alex had left the study Emma had stepped into the passage to better examine the art that was hung there. At first it seemed surprising that Alex would collect art at all, but as she looked at each piece the collection seemed to reflect him perfectly.

They weren't expensive pieces, bought as an investment. Nor were they a show of his wealth or status. They were parts of him—parts of a whole.

There were many paintings reflecting water. A river or an ocean. A lot of them seemed to feature blue prominently, which she guessed might be a colour he was partial to. The huge photographs were scenes from different places across the world, and she remembered what he'd said about wanting Hastings to truly be global.

Emma pulled herself away and went back into the library. It was so inviting, and now she knew it was there it was definitely going to be the place she spent the most time in.

Eager to see what sort of books Alex had in his collection, she started her examination of titles from the first bookshelf, reading the spines as she went.

She didn't get very far. A book she had loved for years caught her eye. Pulling the ladder over, she climbed up two rungs to reach the beautifully embossed hardcover book that was clearly a collector's edition. She ran her fingers over the gold letters on the cover: *The Time Machine*.

It fell open in her hand, to a page that had a magnetic bookmark attached to it. It was a fancy thing. Like something one would receive as a gift. It was leather, and etched in striking patterns with the initials *AJH*. It made her smile that he was reading the same book that had caught her attention.

Emma took it over to the couch, where she curled up with her feet on the cushions. Opening up the first page, she was lost to the fantasy…

After his call, Alex went straight back to the library. Remembering how passionately Emma had spoken of her literacy charity, he knew she wouldn't have left the room. Leaning against the door jamb, Alex watched Emma silently. Having her there fixed a piece of him in place that had been missing for so long, and he recognised how perilous a feeling that was because he just wasn't ready for something like that. It wasn't the way he was wired. But looking at her as he was now, seeing her wrapped in the luxurious throw, brought what he'd thought he knew about himself into doubt.

He noticed that the book she was reading was one

of his favourites. One that he had recently started reading again.

'That's a good book,' he said from the doorway.

Emma looked up with a start. It was as if she had forgotten where she was.

'Sorry, I didn't mean to startle you.' He pushed off the doorframe and joined her on the couch.

'It's fine.' She laughed nervously. 'It's one of my favourites,' she said, turning to the cover.

'Mine too. Sorry I took so long.'

'It's okay. I've been entertained. What's the "J"?' she asked. She smiled at his obvious confusion and held up his bookmark, pointing at his initials.

'James.'

'Never would have guessed.'

'Really?' he asked with amusement.

She laughed, a teasing glint in her eye. 'I would have thought it would be some sort of haughty archaic name, passed down.'

He wasn't taking the bait. 'Sorry to disappoint.' He pulled her throw-covered legs over his lap, holding her against his body. 'I wanted to talk to you about tomorrow.'

'Work?' Emma asked, frowning.

'Work.'

Alex had been picking apart everything she had said to him over the past few days. A picture was beginning to paint itself, of exactly what she was facing. And the reality of the matter was that when Emma went back to the office she would be facing the wrath of her older sister. Unfair as it was, Lauren was, in effect, her boss.

And the look he'd seen on her older sister's face at the masquerade—while amusing at the time—meant that Emma would be facing an untenable situation tomorrow. A situation Alex felt somewhat responsible for.

He never involved himself in the careers of the women he dated, that was true, but he also never got them fired. From what Emma had said of Lauren, it seemed she was waiting for an excuse to be rid forever of the smart younger sister who was very capable of upstaging her but never did.

Emma sighed heavily. 'I'm not going to stress about it, Alexander. Whatever happens, happens. I doubt Lauren is going to retaliate on the day her promotion is announced.'

'So you're just going to stand there and pretend you're happy for her? Even though you were overlooked again?' He could feel his anger rising.

'Yes, because I'm happy for Maddie. At least a part of me is.'

'The other part knows you deserve better.'

Emma shrugged. 'I don't know what I deserve,' she finally responded. 'Better than my family, but that's a low bar.'

He narrowed his eyes. How could she not know what she deserved? She was aware of how hard she worked. Knew what she wanted. Craved the opportunity to be given a chance. So how could she not know? Unless it wasn't so much not knowing what she deserved as it was not knowing her worth.

'Emma…' He made his voice low. Quiet. 'Why don't you think you're good enough?'

Emma didn't answer and looked away.

Alex wouldn't be ignored. He held her chin in a firm grasp, forcing her to look at him. 'What happened? You're not leaving here until you tell me.'

*Why should she?* a voice at the back of his mind asked him. The answer was simple. He wanted to know. Whether he needed to know was immaterial. And Alex always got what he wanted.

'It's nothing. Stupid, really.'

'Tell me anyway.' He knew he'd made it clear that he wasn't going to let it go.

She sighed. 'Not long after I had started working, I dated someone. I wasn't interested in anything serious, but he said all the right things, and did all the right things, and for a moment I contemplated what it would be like to have something real with him. Then he met Lauren. Started ignoring my texts and calls. I found out he'd been seeing her. He chose her. It had always been her. I was just a means to an end.'

*Fool.* How anyone could choose Lauren over Emma was baffling to him. She was by far the most stunning creature he had ever seen. He—Alex, master of control—could barely control himself around her.

'Emma…'

'It's fine. It's in the past. But I should have expected it because my father didn't ever want me either.'

'What do you mean?' Alex was having a hard time reining in his temper now.

'The reason my father hates me so much is because I was—as he so delicately put it—"a mistake my mother refused to fix". He didn't want me.'

A growl left Alex's throat. His eyes turned to shards of ice.

'You have to understand my father is someone who has a plan and sticks to it. Anything outside of that isn't tolerated. Deviations are viciously and swiftly dealt with. He's always been that way.'

Alex remembered what Emma had said about Maddison, and it just made him angrier. His hands were balling into fists, ready to fight a person who wasn't there. 'He was willing to lose you.'

'Yes.'

The matter-of-fact way Emma spoke of all this was even more enraging, because she just accepted it and moved on. As if it was normal. Remained in the family company where she was committed to doing her best.

Once again Alex was moved by the sheer strength of her. And she didn't think she was good enough? That was laughable. He couldn't imagine a more ridiculous notion. If anything, it cemented his decision to walk away at the end of this, because Emma had it all backwards. She needed someone who was deserving of her—and that wasn't him. Could never be.

He moved the hand on her chin to cradle her face. When he spoke his voice was firm. Resolute. 'You don't need any of them. They don't deserve you. None of them do, Emma.'

He picked her up—throw and all—and walked out of the library.

'Where are you taking me?'

'To show you how a beautiful, strong woman should be treated.'

# CHAPTER TWELVE

THE CONVERSATION WITH Emma had been playing on Alex's mind ever since they had left the library. Now he stood at the railing of his rooftop terrace, gazing out at the early-morning light with a cup in his hand. There had to be a way for him to help her. To get her out of a clearly unhappy situation. She was so vivacious, and it tore him apart to see her so downtrodden.

Pressuring her was the last thing he wanted to do, but he had to find a way to give her an out.

And then it occurred to him. Despite the early hour, he pulled out his phone and called in a favour.

The next day found Emma in her office. Her thoughts were constantly being pulled back to the time she'd spent with Alex. It had been perfect. So perfect that she was struggling to concentrate. It was completely unlike her, and she had to get it together, knowing she was being watched more closely than usual.

Her impromptu day off had in fact been noticed by most. But her father had said nothing to her. Well, not verbally. The look he had given her had said it all. It was official. She was now possibly more hated even than her mother.

The day had started with the announcement of Lauren's promotion. Emma had stood behind her sister, impeccably dressed, looking happy and supportive. Pictures had been taken for the company website, with others for the newsletter.

Emma had answered any and all questions aimed at her with grace and confidence. Playing the part of a Brown daughter perfectly. Even when she'd been asked how she felt now that both her sisters were in management positions while she was not, Emma had simply said that the right decisions had been made and that they all had a role to play at Brown Hughs.

She'd given no one any reason to have a gripe with her, and at the end had received the thanks of her mother and Maddison, who seemed to be in a constant state of apology. It wasn't her fault, and Emma was not upset with Maddison.

She found herself often saying, 'Don't worry about it, Maddie.'

After all, Maddison had a job to do, and she couldn't be feeling guilty all the time. They all had to move forward. And perhaps now Emma stood a chance of moving a little higher up the ladder.

It was a busy day, between meetings, approvals and the odd bit of hand-holding, and before Emma knew it she was staring down the barrel of yet another lunch break spent holed up in her office, working. Which was a pity, because it was such a beautiful day. All she wanted was just a little break to feel the sun on her face.

She looked up to see a small commotion outside, and wondered what was going on, but she was busy and had no time to indulge her curiosity. Until there was a knock on her office door.

Emma looked up to see Alex standing in her doorway, looking sinful in a tailored black suit with a white shirt and black tie. A silver tie clip was striking against the dark fabric, and as he dropped his hand a cufflink caught the light. He was perfect. It took her breath away every time he looked at her the way he was doing right now.

Her legs were already carrying her towards him. Magnetised. That was what they were. 'Alexander. What are you doing here?'

He kissed her. A quick but glaring show of his affection. *Mine!* was what it screamed. 'I'm taking you to lunch.'

'I'm swamped,' she said, deflated.

'Make time. You have a meeting,' he said, his voice low.

Her brows knitted together. Unsure of what he had planned, Emma was torn between what she wanted to do and what she had to do. But she did trust Alex, and if he had arranged something, it was worth checking out.

'Let me get my bag.'

Emma locked her computer and slung her handbag over her shoulder. He took her hand in his as they walked out, and she noticed everyone stood a little straighter around him, moving out of his way without him asking. He exuded a power that was *felt*, and she was reminded of the way everyone moved out of his path when they walked through the city.

The doors on the lift slid closed and the people around them kept shooting covert looks their way. It was something Alex seemed completely oblivious to. Perhaps it was something he'd learned to ignore. To Emma, it was new and a little uncomfortable.

She was grateful when they stepped out on the ground floor. Outside, in the bright sunshine, stood his car, parked in the bay just outside the doors.

Alex held the car door open for her and once she was safely inside, closed it and climbed in.

'You look incredible,' he said.

'We had Lauren and Maddison's announcement today,' she said, by way of explanation.

'I know. I saw it online.' He flicked the indicator and pulled out into the street.

'You did?'

'I had to look up the building address.'

'Right… I guess it makes sense that they put it out so quickly.' Emma looked around at the buildings that passed by them, trying to figure out where they were going. 'What's this meeting about?'

An enigmatic smile crept onto his face. 'Do you trust me?'

'Yes,' she said without hesitation. It surprised her how true it was. She trusted Alex.

'Then you'll see.'

Emma let it drop. There was a knot in her stomach that didn't seem to ease, and she knew he could sense it.

'It's worth it. I promise.'

She nodded and forced herself to relax. This would be the only quiet moment she had in her day, so she closed her eyes and enjoyed the feeling of the sun on her skin. It wasn't quite the walk she'd wanted, but it was better because it would be spent with Alex.

He brought the car to a stop in a roadside bay, then opened the door for her. Emma wasn't sure if she would ever get over his chivalry, but she hoped it would never stop. There was no telling when she would get to experience it again once things were over between them.

They walked into a high-end restaurant. The kind that garnered huge followings on social media. The kind you would have a meeting at if you were trying to woo someone. And suddenly she felt as if they were.

There was an immaculately dressed woman in a suit sitting at the table that they were being ushered to.

'Emma, I'd like you to meet Fiona Porter,' Alex said, making the introduction.

She shook the woman's hand. 'Emma Brown...nice to meet you.'

Alex pulled a chair out for Emma before taking his seat beside her. 'Fiona is a director of one of the largest literacy charities in Australia.'

Suddenly it all became clear, and Emma's heart began to race. Alex must have seen the disbelief in her face, and he casually placed his arm around her shoulders. This was the most incredible thing anyone had ever done for her, and Emma was determined not to squander the opportunity.

'Alex tells me you're involved in charity work as well,' Fiona said.

'Yes, I am. I help run a small literacy charity here in Melbourne.' Emma smiled.

'A noble cause. Not a particularly easy one either.' Fiona nodded knowingly.

'No, it isn't. It's always a battle to secure donations. I have to say, I've followed the work of your organisation for a long time. It's what inspired me to get involved.'

'It pleases me greatly to hear that.'

A basket of breads and dips was placed on the table. They waited for the server to leave before continuing their conversation.

'So what does your organisation do, Emma?' Fiona asked.

'We offer classes to teach adults and children…hold book drives…try to collect school materials.'

Emma's heart was beating a frantic tattoo, but she felt the light touch of Alex's thumb caressing the back of her neck and tried to lean into the feeling. She spoke passionately of all that they did and the people she got to meet. How much she enjoyed the work and how they marketed themselves.

Despite the small size of Emma's little organisation, Fiona seemed impressed, and she had Alex to thank. Maybe this was his way of trying to make a difference. Trying to take her away from all the negativity she faced almost every day while still helping others. She'd been able to tell from the moment they met that he hid an enormous heart.

'You say you'd like to give more time to your charity work?' asked Fiona.

'That's right,' Emma replied.

'What do you do in your career?'

Emma launched into a description of her role at Brown Hughs and Fiona seemed more and more interested, asking questions about her academic background and strategic prowess. It was starting to feel a little like an interview.

A waitress came by to take their order. Emma barely registered what she said. She heard Alex's resonating voice. However, all she could concentrate on was the surreal experience she was having.

She was grateful for the fact that Alex had stayed there with her, and that he hadn't just set her up for this meeting, because she was struggling to be her usual composed self even though she tried not to show it.

He'd leaned back in his chair and fixed his intense gaze on Fiona. Something Emma realised he did whenever he was listening intently. People always seemed to respond to it. Now he was in full charm mode, and it gave Emma the time to pull herself together.

They chatted cordially through their meal. But once the coffees had come, Fiona wanted to get down to the matter at hand.

'Emma, as I'm sure you know, we have partnered with many smaller organisations in the past. Provided support where they needed it most. Based on what you've told me, I would love to meet with your colleagues so we can discuss a partnership of our own.'

'That would be amazing!' Emma breathed.

'Of course we would have to look into your organisation first. Can't be too careful.' Fiona smiled.

'Of course. I completely understand,' Emma answered, placing her cup down on the saucer with a clink.

Fiona fished a card out of her bag and handed it to her. 'Give me a call and we can set up a meeting.'

Emma handed one of her own cards over. 'Thank you, Fiona.'

She could scarcely believe her luck. Except it wasn't luck. It was the doing of the one person other than Hannah who wanted to see her happy.

'I hope you'll call soon. We don't want this opportunity to slip through our fingers,' Fiona cautioned.

Emma had already planned to contact the others as soon as she got back to the office. 'Absolutely not.'

'One thing, Fiona...' Alex started. 'These things usually take a while. Can we rush that along?'

Fiona narrowed her eyes at Alex. 'We can get going as soon as Emma is ready. Naturally, since you're here, Alex, I have to tell you how far having some international backing can go in organisations such as ours.'

'I'm well aware, and will have Hastings International's philanthropy division contact you.' Alex turned his attention back to Emma. 'Does that work for you?'

It was a simple question. She recognised it as his way of telling her that she was still the one in control. She could walk away if she wanted, or pursue it, and he would support her. It was her decision to make. His company would be dealing with Fiona's, not hers. There was no pressure on her. And no permanent link to him.

'Yes, definitely.'

* * *

The drive back to her office was quiet. There was a lot for Emma to think on. Excitement was thrumming in her, but so was apprehension. Was she good enough to seize this opportunity? And what would happen if she did? How would her family react if she was involved more heavily with the charity than she already was?

She didn't even realise they had arrived back until Alex opened her door.

'One step at a time,' he said softly.

'Yeah. Just a lot to think about.'

Fiona could change everything. All the projects the charity wanted to get off the ground, all the people they could help—all of it would become easier.

'You can do this, Emma.'

He walked her back to her office.

To her horror, it seemed that news of Alex's presence had reached Lauren. The employees on her floor were all trying to look everywhere except at the tall blonde who had been waiting for her sister. To Emma's relief, her mother arrived just in the nick of time. Helen would be able to ensure that no scene was made.

'Alexander, how nice to see you again,' Lauren said sweetly.

Emma rolled her eyes. *When will you stop?* she thought to herself. They were at work. And they were professionals.

'It's good to see you too, Lauren,' he said politely. 'And, please, it's Alex.'

* * *

Alex was curious to see what sort of game Lauren would play. After all, everyone working on this floor would have either seen or heard that he had kissed Emma. Part of him smiled inwardly at the possessiveness of it all… another part was screaming warnings at him.

'Well, Alex,' she purred, 'it's a surprise to see you here. Wouldn't you rather come up to *my* office? We have a much better meeting space up there.'

Alex wanted to laugh. He heard Emma huff beside him, and wrapped his arm around her waist. 'Oh, I'm not here on business. I just came to drop Emma off after lunch.'

He pressed a kiss to her hair and Lauren's jaw twitched.

'Oh, that's lovely!' Helen said, stepping forward. 'I'm Helen—Emma's mother.'

She extended her hand to him, which he shook warmly. Honestly, he didn't need to be told who she was. Looking into Helen's eyes was almost like looking into Emma's. Like a mirror.

'It's nice to finally meet you, Helen. And I don't mean to be rude, but I do need to rush.' He turned his back on the two women, keeping Emma beside him, and walked her to her office.

For the first time Alex was able to take it in. The space was perfectly neat and orderly. There wasn't a single thing in it that was unnecessary or sentimental. No photos on her desk or pictures on her wall, save for a framed degree which was fixed behind her. The other thing he noticed was how small it was. It would fit into his own office four times at least.

'I expect to see you tonight. I'll text you the code to get in.'

'I'll come straight over after work.'

'Good.' He leaned down to kiss Emma, and she was already meeting his lips halfway. He kissed her long and slow, but pulled away before either of them really wanted to. 'I'll see you later.'

'Alexander?' she called once he was out through the door.

'Yes?'

'Thank you for today.'

He smiled back at her, then left.

# CHAPTER THIRTEEN

THE DRIVE TO the airport took longer than Alex would have liked, but he knew it would be nothing compared to when he was driving back, so he tried his best to remain patient. It would have been easy to send a driver, or have Matt rent a car or use a ride-share, but he had missed his friend. He was probably his only true friend, and Alex wanted to spend as much time with him as he could. They would have time to talk, and Matt would question his sanity.

One morning. That was all the time he'd spent away from Emma, and he could hardly believe how much he craved her touch. After lunch he had been distracted in his meetings. With thoughts of Emma constantly breaking through his normally laser-sharp focus.

Alex checked the time on his watch. He would have to wait only a few minutes for Matt to come through. He parked in the closest available bay to the airport structure. Still dressed in his suit, Alex shrugged off his jacket, depositing it on the back seat, and rolled up his shirtsleeves. Making sure he had the parking ticket, he walked to the pick-up point, keeping an eye out for the tall blond form of his friend.

First class always had its perks, and before the large wave of people disembarking from Economy could pass through, a much smaller number were already exiting the building. That was when Alex saw him. Standing a head taller than most, it was impossible to miss Matt. With the physique of a rugby player, which he'd never lost despite not having played since leaving university, Matt cut an imposing figure. That was before he smiled. He had always had a magnetic personality and people seemed to gravitate towards him. It was easy to be around him.

Matt grinned as soon as he saw Alex, making a beeline for him. 'Alex!'

They hugged and slapped backs.

'It's good to see you, mate.'

Alex had always attracted attention, and he did well to ignore it most of the time, but whenever he and Matt were together it seemed there were ten times as many people looking their way.

The two of them walked back to the car, and Alex stowed his friend's single piece of luggage in the boot. In no time they were back on the road.

Alex had looked forward to Matt's arrival, but what he hadn't counted on was the calm seeing his friend would bring. Between work and his relationship with Emma, Alex had been in a vortex of powerful feelings. It was refreshing to have back the tranquillity that always came from being around Matt.

'What's on the itinerary for tonight?' Matt asked.

'Don't have one. We'll go back to my place and decide from there,' Alex said.

'Sounds good. Just us?'

Alex looked over at his friend and caught the knowing look on his face. It annoyed him sometimes, just how well Matt knew him. 'Emma's coming over.'

Matt didn't comment. Alex knew it was more than a little unusual for him to invite a woman along when standard procedure dictated that they'd cruise the social scene as unattached eternal bachelors. An introduction meant something. Alex knew it would make Matt curious to see what Emma was like for himself. Alex also wanted to see how she got along with Matt. Which meant he was in bigger trouble than he'd realised.

Traffic had come to a crawl and it was already sunset. Alex wondered if Emma was at his flat yet, but he didn't linger on the thought as Matt caught him up on everything going on back in London.

Emma parked in the second empty bay assigned to Alex and carefully picked up the box of cakes she had purchased on her way over.

With a beep, her car was locked, and she made her way to the elevator which was waiting. She pulled out the key to Alex's apartment, still surprised that he had given it to her. It might only be for one night, but it felt as if there was more to the gesture. She hoped she wasn't reading too much into it.

*You are,* a snide voice at the back of her mind commented.

She slid the key into the lock, opening up the door, and stepped into the apartment.

'Alexander?' she called, but there was no response.

Glancing at the time, she figured he would be on his way back. Her heels click-clacked on the wooden floors as she walked through to the kitchen to deposit the sweet treats on the counter. The apartment was eerily quiet. Then she realised there was no music playing. The only time it had been this quiet was when she'd first come over after the masquerade, and then she hadn't really noticed because Alex had seemed to fill the space they were in.

She looked around for something to do, fingers drumming on the countertop. Nothing appealed to her more than making another trip to the library. There she found the book she had been reading, still placed on the couch. Except there was a long copper-coloured bookmark between the pages she had stopped at.

Emma settled in and fell into the story once more. It was at least an hour before she heard voices coming from downstairs, and Alex and Matt finally arrived at the apartment.

Emma flew down the stairs, and the first thing she saw was Alex moving towards her. It had become the most natural thing in the world for them to gravitate towards each other. As if the world had tilted on a different axis.

He kissed her ardently. As if they were being reunited after a great time apart.

'Have you been waiting long?' Alex asked.

'A little over an hour.'

'Sorry, traffic was a nightmare,' he apologised.

She waved it off and he held her against his side.

That was when she saw the man standing with a large black suitcase next to him. As tall as Alex, but much broader, he was an imposing figure with kind green eyes, a handsome face, and a shock of blond hair. Emma thought that these two friends together would set hearts alight wherever they went.

'Emma Brown, this is Matthew Taylor,' Alex said.

'Just Matt.'

Emma smiled.

'It's nice to meet you, Matt.'

'And you, Emma.'

'Before I forget, Alexander, I went to the patisserie. There's a box on the kitchen counter.'

'I like her already.' Matt grinned.

She watched the two men head to the kitchen and inspect the contents of the box. It was a treat to watch Alex like this. She had already seen so many sides to him, and watching him now, with Matt, he seemed younger. More relaxed.

Alex fiddled with his tablet and music came alive overhead.

'You have that on even when you're working?' Matt asked.

'Yeah,' Alex answered.

'Some things never change,' Matt commented, and went back to selecting a cake.

Emma watched the two men keenly. There was something about this evening that niggled at her. It almost felt as though it was some sort of test. That Alex was watching how well she got along with Matt. It didn't make any sense to her that he should want them to get along. Matt seemed very important to him, and Emma was only ever going to be a moment in his life.

A little bit of hope and fear bloomed in her chest that maybe it meant he wanted more time with her. But she closed her eyes and tried to push the feeling away. He had been honest with her, and had never once said this would develop any further. Emma forced herself to remember that. To remember what she wanted too. Fun. No strings. No toxic relationship to follow her around for the rest of her life.

'Emma? Are you okay?' Alex asked.

'Hmm? Oh, yeah. Just thinking about work,' she lied.

She hadn't realised Alex had been watching her, and wasn't sure if he bought the flimsy lie. But he didn't push and for that she was grateful.

Alex presented Matt with the opportunity to talk to Emma alone after dinner, when he was about to make coffee. Throughout the meal, Matt had been watching him with Emma. When they touched, or shared a look or a smile. As if he could tell that whatever was going on between the two of them was different from anything Alex had experienced before.

A loud buzz echoed against the counter. Picking up his phone, Alex frowned as he read through an email.

'I have to take care of something,' he said.

Alex caught Emma's eye and winked. She felt her cheeks turn red, which made his smile grow as he walked away to the study, leaving Matt alone with her.

She finished making the coffees, handing a cup to Matt, who took it to the living room.

'So, Emma, you're involved in charity work?' he said.

'Yes. A small charity. I'm hoping we can partner with a larger organisation, thanks to Alexander.'

She sat cross-legged on the couch opposite him, getting comfortable. She'd had a feeling that he would want to talk to her at some point. After all, friends looked out for each other. She wished sisters did too.

'Oh?'

'Yeah… Alexander has introduced me to the director of a large literacy charity. They seem to like what we do and how we operate.' Emma held the coffee cup in her hands, enjoying its warmth.

'Wow…' Matt said, as if to himself. 'Alex would normally never do that.'

'Help someone out?' she asked sceptically. She was starting to wonder how well Matt knew Alex at all.

'No. He's always willing to help. He's just…disciplined. He has these rules he lives by, and one of those is to never mix business with pleasure. If he got you that meeting he pulled in a favour, and that's not something he would ordinarily do.'

'I've noticed.'

'It means you're different, Emma. I've known Alex for a very long time, and all of this,' he said, gesturing towards her, 'is new. He obviously has strong feelings for you.'

Emma looked at Matt, then dropped her gaze to her cup. Unsure what to say or how much to say.

'I'm going to take a stab and say you do too. You don't have to say it. I can see it. I'm sure Alex does have feelings, but if you're waiting for him to say the words, they're not going to come.'

Emma already knew that. Knew there was going to be an end. It splintered a part of her every time she thought about it, because this was the most alive she had ever felt. Awakened. The fear that she would lose that once he walked out was real. And she wasn't ready to say goodbye to him just yet. But when it did happen she would thank him for helping her find herself. For being *him*. Every moment they'd spent together would be a treasured memory that she would tuck away as she moved on with her life.

Emma cleared her throat, not quite trusting her voice. 'I just want him to be happy. I can see there's things he carries that he doesn't want to talk about. I wish I knew how to help him.'

'Get in line,' Matt said, looking out of the window. There was an unseeing look in his eye. As if he were deep in thought. And then his features set. As if he was resolved in some kind of decision. 'How much have you read about Alex?'

'Actually, nothing since we met at a masquerade. And before that just what was in the news. I didn't want to invade his privacy.'

Matt smiled. It was a soft expression. 'Do you know about his father?'

Emma shook her head. 'He's an earl, and that's as far as I know.'

'And his mother?'

'Just that he doesn't have one.'

'Well, that's half true... Robert Hastings married a woman named Catherine Evans and they had Alex. Robert needed an heir, but Catherine was indifferent. When Alex was born she hated being a mother, had no maternal feelings or even any love for him, and one day she just left.'

Emma listened, horrified that his mother could have done that. It was common knowledge that her mother favoured Maddison, but at least she had been there for Emma in the past, and in a lot of ways still was.

'The thing is, she never left high society. She likes the life. Robert had a reputation as a difficult man in the business world, and Catherine perpetuated rumours that he was the same, if not worse, in private. It was easily believed, so she wasn't cast out. But it isn't the truth. Robert is a hard man to please because of who he is, but he is a good man. So Alex has grown up knowing who his mother is, but she's a complete stranger to him. He's never actually met her.'

'Oh, my God!' Emma covered her mouth. 'That's awful. And cruel.' She uncrossed her legs and got off the couch, moving to stand at the massive window. 'Everything he's said makes so much sense now.'

'What did he say?' Matt asked.

Emma turned around and leaned her back against the large pane of glass. 'He told me he doesn't want the title. He said it leads you to make mistakes and trust the wrong people.'

'That sounds like him. He doesn't ever trust people.'

'But he trusted me,' Emma said softly.

He had shown her as much when he'd spoken to her about his reluctance to accept the legacy that awaited him, and when he'd brought her to his home. The key in her pocket suddenly became an immensely heavy weight.

'He did. Make sure you don't lose that trust. You'll never get it back.'

Matt picked up his coffee and took a long sip. Emma was silent. Reeling from his revelations. It was a clear warning from Matt, but Emma was determined to be what Alex needed, just as he had been for her, for as long as she could.

She couldn't stop thinking about everything Matt had said. It played over and over in her mind like a broken record and, despite wanting to spend another night with Alex, she knew she shouldn't let herself forget exactly what this relationship was. Spending the night here with Matt around would feel like a lot more than either of them wanted. So she stole a moment alone with Alex just as he was about to leave his study.

She pushed him back in and closed the door behind her. He clearly knew what she was after. Pressing her back against the door, his hands on either side of her head, Alex kissed her with a ferocity that promised so much pleasure. The air was sucked out from around them and all that was left was a vacuum, thick with desire.

When she plunged her hands under his shirt Alex groaned, pressing his hardness against her. Making her whimper. But Emma broke the kiss.

'I have to go.'

'Tease.'

The smile she gave him was nothing short of wicked.

Alex let her leave, cursing himself as he did so, because all he really wanted right now was to take her to bed. He stood at the rail of his rooftop terrace, with the sea air cooling his overheated face and helping him find some sort of equilibrium after that kiss.

Matt came up beside him, leaning on his elbows, taking in the spectacular sight of night-time in Melbourne at the water's edge. 'What's going on, Alex?'

'With what?'

'You and Emma.'

Alex snapped his gaze to his friend, but Matt's face was a blank mask. There was neither hope nor judgement. It was just a simple question from the person who knew him better than anyone else.

'Nothing is going on. We've agreed to have some fun.'

'Alex, you know I love you, right? But you're an idiot.'

Alex couldn't help the smile that broke through. He'd missed Matt's particular brand of caring.

'Bloody hell, mate… You feel something for her.'

Alex couldn't lie to Matt. He did care for Emma. But that didn't mean he would change the course of his life for her. He had made it perfectly clear what he was looking for, and he felt no guilt because Emma wanted the same. It was possible that she was as jaded as he was—except he wasn't going to tell Matt that. Emma's secrets were his to keep.

'I'm not in it for the long haul, Matt.'

'Then what are you doing? She's not the only one growing attached. You are too. Have you considered that maybe you wouldn't fare as badly as your father?'

Matt never pulled any punches. Not with Alex. For their entire lives they had been totally honest with each other. A difficult conversation was never avoided for fear of how the other would react.

'I know I won't, because I'm not going to commit.'

'That's a lie and you know it. You have a title to think about,' Matt pushed.

'I don't know what to tell you. We're having fun, and when it's done we'll go our separate ways. She knows the score.'

'I know you're lying to yourself.' Matt shook his head, his tone softening. 'Whether you want to or not, one day you will have to accept everything you're trying to push away right now, Alex.'

Maybe Matt was right, but his legacy didn't mean as much to Alex as it did to everyone else. So what if he never had a family? The manor, the title—they meant very little to him. How could he set any store by them when it couldn't keep his family together? When that burden caused nothing but pain. Alex refused to put himself through that. There was no room for love in his life and there wouldn't ever be. Of that he was certain. Alex enjoyed his life as it was right now.

*Right now, you have Emma*, said a voice within him. He stubbornly ignored it.

'We're going out,' Alex said to Matt.

He needed to get away from his apartment to clear his head. Because everything in it made him think of Emma.

# CHAPTER FOURTEEN

EVEN WITH MATT spending the next two weeks at Alex's apartment, Emma found time to be with him. She had tried to keep her distance, but after just two days neither she nor Alex had been able to resist the urge to be with each other.

She still knew it was time that Alex needed with his friend, and that being around the two of them felt too much as if their relationship could be something more, so Emma kept away as much as she could—even though it often felt as if she couldn't breathe for missing Alex. That worried her more than anything.

So when Matt suggested the three of them go out, Emma invited Hannah along as a buffer. But Matt was so taken with Hannah that Alex and Emma were soon forgotten, allowing them to slip away. They were so desperate for each other that his lips were on hers before she could even get out of the car.

When it finally came time for Matt to leave, everyone was sorry to see him go.

Emma went to shake his hand, but he pulled her in for a hug, and once she got over the surprise she found the familiarity endearing. It was a kind of warmth she had never truly encountered in her own family, and even though Matt was just a friend, by Alex's own admission he was as good as a brother.

'Take care of him,' Matt whispered in her ear.

Emma managed to contain her shock. She had been certain he knew that she and Alex had an expiration date, despite what he had told her.

All she said in reply was, 'Take care of yourself, Matt.'

Alex was next to embrace his friend, and once they'd bade each other farewell he led Emma away, giving Matt a private moment with Hannah.

'I want you to stay with me tonight,' he told her.

'Are you trying to make up for lost time?' Emma laughed.

'Yes.'

There was an intensity in his eyes that drew her in. She was lost in the sea of them.

'I'll be there.'

And she was—as soon as she was done with her evening's commitments to the charity.

Alex immediately took her to bed, making love to her over and over again until they were both utterly spent.

When she woke he wasn't in bed with her—as she had come to expect. She readied herself for work and then went searching for him in the large apartment. He was in the gym, and she had to stop herself from salivating at the sight of him. A towel hung around his neck, and his shirtless torso was drenched in sweat.

He pushed away the hair sticking to his forehead as he placed large weights on a metal rack.

Catching sight of her in the mirror, he smiled.

'I hope I didn't interrupt,' she said.

Alex was tapping the screen of his fitness watch. 'No, I've just finished up.'

Emma stepped over the threshold of the room, walking towards him. Her delicate finger traced a line along his glistening pectoral. A gentle touch. He closed his eyes.

'Emma, we have to talk,' he said softly.

'I know what you're going to say, Alexander.'

The past two weeks didn't mean anything. It couldn't. They had simply had a good time. Emma wouldn't let herself believe anything other than that.

She looked around at all the workout equipment. This room was better equipped than some professional gyms. 'Why do you work yourself so hard?'

'For control. I need it in every aspect of my life,' he said, watching her. Her hands were still on him.

'Is it because you want to control who enters and leaves your life? How you feel about it? How you respond to it?'

'Emma...'

He had never said her name like that. She knew it was a warning to drop the subject. He wasn't going to discuss his mother with her.

'It might not be so bad to let someone into your heart,' she said, holding his gaze. It was careful. Guarded. No emotion to be seen. No weakness for her to read.

'I don't have one,' he said flatly.

It was a statement. And suddenly there was a buzzing in her ears from the rage she felt for a woman she had never met. Emma didn't push. She didn't have a right to. But she hated that shut-off expression on his face.

Her hands travelled around his neck and into his hair, tugging his face down to hers. The moment their lips connected she felt the steel-like stiffness leave his body as his tongue plundered her mouth, making her moan. And then he took her up against the mirror.

Alex couldn't remember the last time he had enjoyed himself so much. Having Emma around just felt right. He'd wanted to see how she would fit into his life, and so far he was running out of reasons to push her away. Not that he wanted to. But he *had* to.

Confusion wasn't a feeling he often felt, and it was not one he was enjoying. He couldn't forget the conversation he had with Matt, and was scared that all the time they were spending together would start meaning something more to Emma. That the fact he craved her touch meant something more.

He sat in his office, tossing a little ball in the air as he pondered through all the thoughts in his head. Sorting through work and home and Emma.

He had a ball like it in all his workspaces, but it was placed back on the desk as he figured out the solution to a work problem. Just as his fingers reached the keys of his laptop, his phone rang.

'Alexander Hastings,' he answered.

'Good evening, Mr Hastings. This is Dr Bernard from the Fairmont Hospital.'

Alex's blood ran cold. 'What's happened?'

'Your father has had a heart attack.'

Alex was already on his feet, storming out through the door.

'He is stable, but he will have to remain in our care for a few days.'

He bashed the elevator button. It was taking too long to come up. Just as he moved towards the stairs, the ding informed him that the car had arrived. He rushed in, hitting the button for the car park.

'Okay, thank you. Keep me informed of everything. I'll be there as soon as I can. Probably very early in the morning.'

Alex barely heard what was said after that. He shoved his phone in his pocket and threw open the car door. He hurriedly climbed in and shut it, much harder than he meant to. Much harder than he should. He ran his fingers through his hair and punched the steering wheel. He felt as if his lungs were being squeezed as he fought to keep the dread at bay.

With squealing tyres, his car left the space.

Barely an hour had passed since Alex had received the call from the doctor, but he was already at Essendon Airport, climbing aboard the Hastings International private jet with single-minded determination. He had to leave. Right now. And he kept up a mantra in his head of what he had to do. Alex could think of nothing else.

Operating on autopilot, Alex was silent. He said nothing to the pilot, or even to his cabin crew when they came through offering refreshments. Fear had a stranglehold on him. It was a vice around his lungs, squeezing the air out.

It was an unbearably long flight and despite arriving in the early hours of the morning, Matt was there to meet him.

He drove straight to the hospital and before he could bring the car to a complete stop, Alex was already getting out. His heart was hammering in his chest, terrified of what he would find.

Practically running, he went up to the private ward. The doctor was waiting, ready to talk to him before he could enter his father's room.

'Dr Bernard?' Alex asked. He hadn't slept at all on the flight, and it felt as if he was staying awake through sheer will.

She nodded. 'Mr Hastings,' she said in greeting.

'How is my father?' Though Alex seemed in control, the only tell that he was afraid to hear the answer was the clenched fist at his side.

'Tired. He's had what we call a non-ST elevation myocardial infarction—or a mild heart attack. There should be no lasting damage, but he will need a change in diet and lifestyle. A good exercise regime. And he must avoid stress. But all in all I think he will be fine. He will need to take it easy for the next few weeks while he recovers.'

Alex's shoulders sagged in relief. 'And his treatment?'

'I will be prescribing a list of medications. I think he should be out of here in a day or two, but he'll need to have constant follow-ups with his cardiologist.'

'He doesn't have one. Hasn't needed one before. Since you've treated him, I'd like him to be seeing you,' Alex said, instantly feeling more like himself. 'And if you give me the prescription, I will have it filled. May I see him now?'

'You can go ahead—but don't wake him.'

Alex walked into a room that was beautifully decorated. Had it not been for the medical equipment, it would have rivalled a luxury hotel. He'd expected darkness. For his father to be asleep. But the bedside light was on and he was reading something on his phone. It took a moment for him to notice his son at the door.

'Alex?' he said with surprise, putting his phone down.

'Dad.' With relief coursing through him, Alex showed more emotion than he ever had in his life. He walked straight to his father and engulfed him in a hug.

'What are you doing here?' he asked.

'Seriously? You gave me a scare!' Alex seemed to be caught somewhere between anger and hysterical laughter.

Robert Hastings took his son's hand in his. 'I'm so happy to see you, but you didn't need to come all this way.'

'Of course I did.' Alex sank into the armchair beside the bed.

'Did you speak to the doctor?'

'I did,' Alex said. 'And we'll be making some changes.'

His father rolled his eyes and Alex narrowed his. 'Don't give me that look. It's time you completely stepped back from the company.'

Walking into this room, he'd felt as if he'd let out a breath he had been holding in for nearly a day. Now Alex almost felt light-headed. The moment he'd received the news all he'd been able to think about was how he wasn't ready to lose his father. His only real family. He had prayed—actually prayed…something he hadn't ever done—to anyone who might hear him for his father to be okay. Alex would have done anything. And now that he was here changes would be made whether his father approved or not.

'Alex—'

'I don't want to hear it, Dad. You need to remove all the stress from your life. You're going to take some time out at the manor. You can come back to London for your follow-ups. And we're getting someone to help you recover.'

'You want me to get a nurse?'

'Yes.'

'Alex, I have things to do…'

'I can take care of all of that.'

The two Hastings men stared each other down, but it was Robert who gave in first. His son's stubborn streak surpassed even his.

'Fine. There's a charity dinner the day after tomorrow. You can start with that.'

'I'll attend in your stead, and when you're discharged I'll take you to the country myself.'

'Alex, you do realise that I'm your father?'

'Yes—and I only have one of those, so I'm going to make sure he takes care of himself and outlives me out of spite.'

It was the first smile Alex had cracked in over a day. The terror was gone, the fear had left his eyes, and he was himself once again.

'Son, you need to calm down.'

'Like hell I do.' Alex took a breath as his father's fingers tightened around his. 'I think I need to let you get some sleep. I take it the dinner invitation is at the house?'

'Yes, in my study.'

'Okay. Would you like me to bring you anything to-morrow?' Alex asked as he stood.

'Now that you mention it—'

'I mean books…that sort of thing.'

'Anything, son.'

'Get some sleep, Dad.'

Alex kissed his father's head then left. Happy to see the light go out in the room as he walked away.

Alex fell into bed that night completely exhausted. Not a single thought was spared for the fact that he was in his London apartment after months of being away. It could have been a tiny room in the middle of nowhere for all he cared. Nothing in his life had prepared him for the feeling seeing his father in that hospital bed had brought. Knowing that Robert would be fine was a small comfort, but he was being confronted with his mortality, and everything Alex had been denying all these years suddenly loomed so large in front of him he could barely breathe.

Earl Hastings. He wasn't ready.

With a knot in his gut that wouldn't let up, he fell into a fitful sleep.

# CHAPTER FIFTEEN

TWO DAYS.

It had been two days since Emma had heard from Alex. No calls. No messages. No promises of the pleasure that awaited her. This must be it. What she had been dreading for weeks. The inevitable end.

There had been no promises of long goodbyes when they'd started this. All it was meant to be was a release. Exploring their chemistry. And then it would be over. That was the promise Alex had made to her. Nothing more.

Emma walked to her office in a daze. Not willing to admit it, having their relationship end so abruptly hurt. She wasn't upset with Alex. He'd kept his word after all. All she wished was that he had told her instead of just disappearing. Especially after all that they'd shared. All that he had awakened in her.

Despite everything, a tiny part of Emma wondered what it would have been like if she and Alex were different people. If they could have had more than just a few mind-blowing nights. If life hadn't ripped their hearts to shreds, could they have had a future?

She flopped into her chair with a huff. Those thoughts wouldn't help her, or fill the hole that was growing in her chest because she missed him. Maybe a part of her always would.

There was a small blossom of hope that maybe she would get to see him again. After all, he had promised Fiona that Hastings International would provide her charity with financial support through their philanthropy programme.

But even if she saw him it wouldn't be the same. The passionate kisses, the explosive chemistry would be gone. It was over.

Throwing herself into work, Emma refused even to look at her phone for the rest of the day. Keeping busy was the way she would deal with this, because whatever she'd shared with Alex wouldn't bow her or break her, it had only built her up.

It was late in the afternoon and the office had mostly emptied. There were only two lights on in the entire floor—hers and her manager's. Emma was exhausted. She tried not to think of Alex, but he kept creeping into her thoughts. Stealing away her concentration with memories of their time together. The night at the Skydeck would be one she would treasure to her last breath.

The phone that she had been ignoring all day sprang to life, and when she saw the caller she was caught between concern and confusion.

'Hi, Matt,' she answered.

'Emma, something's happened.'

She tried to suppress a sob, her heart breaking for Alex as Matt quickly told her all that had happened.

An image of his father, the man he so greatly admired lying in a hospital bed filled her mind. *'It was just my father and I,'* he had said to her.

And then guilt ripped through her. She'd thought he was done with her. That they were at an end. When he probably hadn't even thought about her at all. He would have been consumed with terror. He needed her. That was why Matt had called her, she realised.

'I'll be on the next flight out.'

Emma rushed to Greg's office, convincing him to give her time off. It was an emergency, after all.

And the moment he agreed, she was running for the elevator.

The flight took an agonisingly long time. It was more than enough time for her to question if she was doing the right thing.

Would Alex want her there? They weren't in a relationship.

Then she realised it didn't matter. Because he *needed* her. She was going to be with him. To help him carry this load, however heavy it turned out to be.

She could do that for him.

Alex entered the bright banqueting hall. It was spectacular. With red and gold carpets and carved wooden walls, it was like stepping back in time. The rows of hanging chandeliers cast a golden glow over everything, making it seem like a scene out of a fairy tale.

There were people everywhere in stunning outfits and expensive jewellery. He didn't care. He was numb to all of it. The ridiculousness of having to be at a party full of rich sycophants while his father lay in a hospital bed sickened him.

This wasn't his scene. It never had been.

It wasn't like the wild parties that he and Matt had enjoyed. Two bachelors without a care in the world. Where his title didn't matter. Where he didn't have to worry about a casual hook-up thinking there might be something more.

From where he stood now, even those held little appeal. All he wanted to do was drive to the hospital and sit in that chair beside his father. But he couldn't. Atlas. That was who he felt like. With the obligation of his family title bearing down on him like the weight of the world on his shoulders. But for his father, he would endure it.

Alex walked through the sea of bodies, not seeing hide nor hair of Matt. He made his way to the bar, still fighting that empty feeling he carried since leaving Melbourne.

After ordering a drink, he leaned against the bar— and then the world was tugged out from under him.

Emma.

There she was, standing at the entrance.

An absolute vision.

Alex thought he had to be hallucinating, but then his feet were carrying him towards her. That emptiness in him was closing a little more with each step and he knew she was really there.

She walked up to him with that smile that dimmed everything around her. 'Hello, Alexander,' she said softly.

He didn't answer. All he did was take her face in his hands and kiss her with desperation and longing. She had come all this way for him, and he realised right then just how much he had needed her. From the moment he'd got that call, every thought had been about getting to his father. He felt like a fool, because now that he had Emma in his arms he felt centred again.

Resting his forehead against hers, he said, 'You're here.'

'Of course I am.' Her hands came to his chest. 'I'm so sorry about your father...but I'm here now. We'll get through it together.'

'Emma...' he breathed.

It was all he could say. No one had ever stopped their world spinning just to be there for him. He had always accomplished everything alone. It was why he was so single-minded at times. Having Emma drop everything to support him at a time like this made him want to weep.

He suddenly realised that people were staring, so he offered her his arm and then saw Matt and his sister Sarah entering. He offered his friend a smile. Matt simply winked back in response.

Despite her upbringing, Emma felt like an interloper amongst these people. Still, she held her head high and wouldn't let anyone shake her confidence. Especially after Alex had walked towards her with an expression that had morphed from a scowl to disbelief to...happiness?

Emma couldn't deny it any longer. She was there to support the man she loved.

*Loved.*

When she'd stepped into his embrace, every head had turned to look at them. Emma didn't care. And when she looped her arm in his it felt right. As if this was where she belonged. Even the warning she usually kept close, telling herself she shouldn't entertain these thoughts, was cast aside. None of it mattered. Not right now.

She was dressed in a long-sleeved blood-red velvet dress that hugged her body and flared out below her hips, falling like a curtain to the floor. The deep V neck exposed her long neck and fair chest, but still remained entirely demure. Her hair was swept back and straight, and silver and diamond drops hung from her ears. She knew she stood out from the crowd.

'Ravishing,' Alex said looking down at her.

But to Emma he looked just as good. In a black tux, he made all the words she wanted to say die on her tongue. Instead, she ran her fingers over the stubble on his cheek and pressed a kiss to his jaw.

Wanting her closer, Alex moved to wrap his arm around her waist. He was afraid she might disappear, as if this was all a trick of his overstressed mind, and he wasn't going to let her go. Even when Matt and his sister approached them and made the necessary introductions.

Emma thanked Sarah, who had lent her the dress, and then the four of them seated themselves at one of the many round tables spaced out around the floor. A section had been cleared as a dance floor, before a small stage with musicians playing various string instruments sitting upon it.

An auction was held, during which Alex paid an exorbitant amount of money for a piece of art that would likely be left behind in his flat in London when they went back to Melbourne. He didn't mind. As much as he hated these events, he always approved of the fund-raising.

During dinner he paid little attention to everyone around them. Emma was with him, and he hadn't realised until now how much he needed her. Scarcely believing that he hadn't once thought to call her, Alex held her hand tightly now, not wanting to let go for even a second.

'What is it?' Emma asked as she caught him staring at her for what must have been the hundredth time that evening.

'You look beautiful,' he said, but it wasn't what he wanted to say.

He wanted to say how grateful he was that she was here. How hollow he had been feeling. How she made him not care even a little about who else was in this room tonight. He just couldn't get the words out.

Once all the plates had been cleared, and the mingling had begun in earnest, Sarah insisted on introducing Emma to some of the other ladies.

A group of the most elegant women Emma had ever seen stood near a window, each with a flute of champagne in her hand. Sarah was busy giving Emma a crash course on who each woman was, and any titbit of information that would help her fit in. Emma was grateful. Sarah made her feel welcome in this world, and it was nice to have found someone so friendly.

The two of them approached the group, who welcomed them with smiles. That was until Emma saw a beautiful tall blonde woman, who reminded her very much of Lauren in the way she held herself.

'Catherine,' Sarah said.

*Catherine?* Emma thought to herself. *Could it be?*

When she saw the smile on Sarah's face falter, she knew it was Alex's mother. Emma was suddenly consumed with a red-hot rage that she tried to bottle up. Alex was just a few meters away, and yet here was his mother who didn't even care.

'I heard you weren't coming tonight,' Sarah said sweetly, quickly recovering.

'Where else would I be, dear?'

Sarah didn't answer. Instead, she looped her arm through Emma's. 'This is Emma. She's visiting from Melbourne.'

Everyone welcomed her. Each had a different question to ask, and she happily answered all of them without missing a beat. Remembering her fine manners, it was easy to slip into conversation with them, but once the dance floor opened up one by one they left to join their partners, until it was just Catherine, Sarah and Emma.

'We should get back too, Emma.'

Sarah tried to turn them around, but Catherine had different ideas.

'So you're Alexander's date,' Catherine said, in a haughty way.

'Yes, I am,' Emma replied.

Sarah exchanged a look with her, telling her that unfortunately they couldn't just walk away. Making a scene was out of the question.

'Just his latest conquest then,' she said snidely. 'Someone should warn you: the apple didn't fall very far from the tree, I'm afraid.'

'It would seem that you aren't very familiar with Alexander at all,' Emma said pleasantly. She looked over her shoulder and saw him staring at them. His eyes were like ice. 'I have to get back to my date. Have a good evening.'

The two of them walked away, with Sarah grumbling under her breath, 'I hate that woman.'

'Matt told me a little about her. She didn't want to be a mother.'

'Oh, she's remarried now,' Sarah said. Seeing the look on Emma's face, she continued. 'Society at large may now be open-minded and progressive, but you have to keep up appearances in these circles. Her husband doesn't care what she does, and she feels the same, as long as they appear together when they need to.'

Emma didn't like the sound of that at all, but they had arrived at the group surrounding Matt and Alex and the two women split apart.

Alex's lips came down to her ear. His arm wrapped around her possessively. 'What did Catherine say to you?'

Emma shook her head. 'Nothing important.'

Alex studied her face. But whatever he was thinking about was pushed aside as he asked her to dance with him. With her hand in his, Alex swept her onto the dance floor. The sweet melody drifted over them and he pulled her close, leading in his effortless way. Swaying to the music, wrapped in a bubble… This was where Emma wanted to be. In his arms.

'Emma?' he said, in a voice that caressed her like smooth velvet.

'Yes?'

'I'm happy you're here.'

She beamed up at him and then tucked her head into his shoulder. There was a part of her that had worried that he didn't actually need her. Seeing him now, hearing his words, made every second spent travelling so very worth it.

'Would you like to leave?' he asked.

'Can we?'

He kissed her forehead. 'Of course. I can't wait to get you home.'

# CHAPTER SIXTEEN

THE NEXT DAY Alex took Emma to the hospital so he could fetch his father and drive him to the family manor. Robert had flat-out refused to be wheeled out to the black Range Rover that his son had arrived in, already loaded with bags and the exercise equipment Alex had procured to assist in his recovery, and Emma waited patiently while Alex fussed, making sure his father was properly buckled in before he walked her to his low, sleek Porsche and handed over his key.

'It's fast. Be careful,' he instructed.

'It will be fine, Alexander. Relax. I have the satnav already set and I'll follow right behind you, I promise.'

He knew he was being a little obsessive; it was just that he needed Emma to be safe. There would be no relaxing until they all arrived at Greenfield House. Alex kissed her sweetly, then opened the door for her. Once she was in, he closed it. Emma started the car with a throaty roar and gave him a thumbs-up.

Alex climbed into the large SUV and pulled out of the parking area, checking his mirrors to ensure Emma was following.

It took them a little under two hours to reach the long gravel driveway of the manor, which crunched under his tyres. Despite the icy weather, the place looked beautiful. Tall trees lined the long drive, hiding the dwelling from sight. But as he rolled forward, the immense redbrick house was gradually revealed. Its Georgian architecture was beautiful, with white accents on the windows and pillars popping brightly against the red background and green scenery.

Emma was absolutely captivated by the house. She brought Alex's car to a stop, and when she got out revelled in the tranquillity. In front of the house, Alex and a member of staff were already pulling the bags out of the back of the Range Rover and carrying them up the steps into the house.

When Emma entered, she thought she had gone back in time. The walls were panelled in dark wood and a grand, carved staircase took centre stage in the hall. The only word she could think of to describe the place was regal. It had an old-world glamour that she only ever experienced when she'd travelled or read about it. There was so much history here. These walls must hold generations of memories.

She followed Alex upstairs. He had deposited his father's bags in a large master suite that had its own sitting area and now he led her to his own, situated on the same floor, but at the far corner of the house and overlooking the grounds.

He grinned at her as he put the bags down. 'Gives us a bit of privacy.'

She giggled at his flirty wink. Following him out and along the many corridors, it started to dawn on Emma exactly who Alex was. What his life was meant to be. The large portraits of his ancestors didn't help the anxiety blooming in her. He wasn't ordinary, and suddenly their life in Melbourne seemed like make-believe. More evidence of why this could never be anything but a temporary fixation.

All of a sudden he seemed further from reach than he ever had, and she was even more determined to make the most of this while she could. And when she was old and grey, alone with her cats, she would have memories to keep her heart warm.

The melancholy was hard to push away.

Alex left her when they went downstairs, and went to the room where the nurse he had hired had already set up a gym. The cook was there, listening carefully to the nurse's instructions as she handed her a list of ingredients that were permitted and those that were now forbidden.

Emma was deep in conversation with his father when Alex came back into the living room.

'Emma, shall we go for a walk?' he asked. 'You'll need your coat,' he said from the door.

'Enjoy it,' his father called as they left the room.

Alex already had his heavy charcoal pea coat on, and waited at the front door as she ran upstairs to fetch a puffy jacket.

'Ready?' he asked, watching her jog down the stairs.

'Yup.'

He held the door open and out she stepped. The cold bit at her cheeks. They trudged down the steps onto the gravel, then Alex stopped. Curling his lip over his teeth, he whistled loudly and waited. From around the side of the house two large fluffy dogs bounded towards them. Tails wagging frantically, they jumped up, trying to get as close to Alex as possible.

'Hey guys!' He patted their heads and scratched their chins. 'Okay, that's enough. Sit!' he commanded, and instantly they listened. 'Good boys.' He looked at Emma. 'This is Clifford and Gatsby.'

Emma remembered the Airedale Terriers he had told her about and she had wished she could meet them. Now she was.

Holding her hand out to them, she let both dogs sniff, and once again their tails began to wag. 'They're beautiful!'

He grasped her hand in his and turned to walk away. 'Clifford, Gatsby—let's go.'

The dogs were at their side as they followed the path that crunched beneath their feet, through a copse of trees.

'It's so lovely here,' Emma said, looking out over an empty paddock. 'Horses?'

'Yes. To both.'

'But you don't like coming here?' Emma looked at Alex, who was watching the dogs run ahead.

'Not particularly. When I was young and Matt would come, it was fun. There was plenty of mischief to get up to.' He smiled fondly at the memory. 'But there's a lot I don't like being reminded of here.'

'I understand. Especially after meeting Catherine.'

'What did she say to you?' he asked.

His feelings were masked but his eyes spoke volumes. Emma could see hurt and anger burning in them.

'She just made a snide comment,' Emma said.

Alex let go of her hand and stuck his in his jacket pockets. Emma followed suit.

'Which was?'

'I don't want to upset you, Alexander.'

'*You* won't.'

Emma sighed, and told him exactly what Catherine had said. Saying the words to him now made her just as angry as she'd been on hearing them the night before. Catherine was cruel, and Emma could only imagine how it must have made Alex feel to see her.

*You understand what it's like. You can help him,* that inner voice said.

Alex pulled on her sleeve, forcing her to stop. 'You know that's not true.'

'I know. I told her she doesn't know you at all.'

'And you know who she is?'

'I do. Although when you said you didn't have a mother I assumed…'

'She was dead?' he said, without the tiniest hint of emotion.

'Yes.'

Alex moved to the paddock, folding his arms on the high white fence. His gaze was far off. 'Dead or alive, it makes no difference.'

Emma climbed onto the fence, sitting on top of it to face Alex. 'Would you like to talk about it?'

She could tell his teeth were clenched behind his lips. That would be a no, then. 'Whatever she says is a lie anyway. But I think your dad is amazing. And so are you.'

Alex still wasn't looking at her.

'You know, growing up, I wished that I had a father like yours,' she told him. 'I would read story books about earls and dukes and pretend the characters were my family. I'm not proud of it, but sometimes I wished that my dad would just go away. But then I'd realise what that would mean and I'd feel guilty.'

She watched the dogs run around and chase each other, oblivious to the cold.

'It's hard when you have to deal with parents like mine. And, of course, you can never say anything bad about it—not that you'd want to anyway. Everyone sees what you have—a big house and money—but they never see what you don't have,' she said sadly.

Alex was watching her carefully now. Silent.

'And the biggest of that is faith. Faith that things will work out and be okay. For as long as I can remember my parents were at each other's throats. They would bicker constantly. Sometimes I would put a pillow over my head to block them out, and then I asked to move my bedroom. It was quieter in the new room, even though it was the smallest room in the house. After that the affairs started. My father didn't even bother trying to hide it. And I swore that would never be me.'

She looked at Alex, who held so much warmth and

love in his eyes. And she wanted him to stop looking at her like that because he couldn't ever be hers. But she wanted to get lost in those blue pools anyway.

She looked away. It was easier just to keep talking. And the rolling hills were a beautiful distraction.

'It got a little better when Maddison was young, but we're right back where we were again now. At least she has me. Lauren doesn't seem to care as long as she and my father get their way. It's a pretty sad way to live, don't you think?'

Alex moved to stand between her legs. Holding on to her, he set her on her feet and pulled her against his body. Hugged her tightly. For a moment the place he stood in didn't feel like a prison. For the first time it felt like home.

After the terror of his father's heart attack, and days of constant worry, Alex didn't have the strength in that moment to push Emma away. For just this one time he wanted to feel peace. It was as if his lifestyle of beautiful women and doing what he wanted when he wanted to, always the armour to protect himself, meant nothing. Could be cast away.

'I'm sorry.'

It was all Alex could say, because it was true. He was sorry that she'd had to endure all that for so long. Sorry he hadn't met her earlier. Sorry that she had to be strong out of necessity. Sorry that they couldn't be more to each other.

'You deserve better.'

'So do you,' Emma said, her voice muffled by his coat. 'We should probably start making our way back.'

'Yeah, we should.'

He whistled to the dogs, who walked beside the couple as Alex showed Emma around the estate. Through the stables, past the enormous garage, along the garden paths. She was delighted to see the maze and Alex walked her through it, having long ago figured out all the ways out.

When they got back to the house the dogs made a beeline for the fireplace, settling in front of the hearth. His father was seated in an armchair, waiting for their arrival.

'Alex, I want you to go back to London,' he said, when the two of them had settled down. 'I appreciate all you're doing, son, and I'm willing to do as you ask. But for me to relax, I need you to be close to the company.'

'Dad…'

'I already know everything you're going to say, but I'm being well taken care of here.'

'Robert, we just want to make sure your recovery goes well,' Emma said.

'My dear, I know that. But I also know my son hates it here. He needs the city, and the company needs him there. If you want me to be stress-free, you'll go back.'

Alex laughed. He knew there was no point arguing with the man. 'We'll leave tomorrow—but we will be back before we return to Melbourne.'

'Lovely.'

'And remember, everyone is reporting to me…so I'll know what's going on here,' Alex said sternly.

'I'd expect nothing less, son.'

* * *

Emma and Alex spent all the time they could with his father that evening. Stories were told of what their lives had been like over the years, and Emma found out that Robert had always been a stern and imposing man, but had loosened up considerably when Alex took the reins at the company.

Despite what they said, Emma could see how much Robert loved his son. Watching them, she couldn't help but smile. It was sweet to see how much Alex cared for his father. He was, after all, the only family Alex really had.

Alex caught her eye, and she stopped breathing at the look he gave her. Moments later they were up in his room, with Alex creating a new memory for this house to hold.

# CHAPTER SEVENTEEN

ALEX AND EMMA didn't leave for London until late the next day. For the first time Alex felt the manor wasn't an imposing prison for his soul, waiting for him like an over-eager jailer. The sun beamed down over the rolling hills, and even though it didn't warm them, Alex wanted to enjoy it for just a little while.

Soon enough the life in this manor would claim him, and the freedom he craved would be gone. When that happened he would at least have these two days to think on. A small reminder that once upon a time, these walls had held laughter and that three-letter word he yearned for. Fun.

When they arrived back in London, Alex realised how well his father knew him. He had been right. Alex *did* need the city. As soon as he stepped into his flat he felt the tension that had pulled him so taut ebb away.

Alex didn't show Emma around his flat that night. He simply took her to bed. And that was where they stayed until he blearily opened his eyes and needed a moment to figure out where he was. Then everything came rushing back and he was suddenly wide awake.

He ran a hand through his tousled hair. The room was still dark, and after finding the control pad on his side table he pressed the button that would raise the blinds. The sky beyond the large window looked like steel. He missed the sunshine.

Taking a moment before he looked over at the sleeping woman beside him, Alex still couldn't quite believe that Emma had flown all this way to be with him and expected nothing in return. Her hair fanned over the pillow. Light was falling over the curve of her breasts, the sheet only just hiding her nipples from view. This woman—this tremendously beautiful woman—had him stirring without even trying.

Emma was still fast asleep. He rolled onto his side with his head propped up on his arm. She looked so peaceful that he didn't want to wake her. But need coursed through him so painfully that he couldn't bear not to.

'Emma,' he said softly, brushing her hair away from her face.

Her brows knitted together as she slowly woke, blinking away the sleep from her eyes. 'Morning...'

She bathed him in a glorious smile and he felt his heart clench. Still stroking her hair, for a moment he wondered how he would ever walk away from her. Why he would want to. Their attraction showed no sign of dissipating. Frustrating. That was what it was. Because it seemed ridiculous that he should deny himself. But what if this attraction never died? Then what? He didn't care for strings. For relationships. For love.

Emma leaned into his touch, her eyes closed. His

hand slid from her hair, grazing her cheek as his thumb traced the line of her lips. Slowly, she opened her blue-grey eyes wide. The embodiment of winter. Those eyes would haunt him for the rest of his life.

Something shifted in them, as if she'd suddenly re-alised that for once he was there with her in bed. Alex had been so careful. Even at the manor he had always woken before she had. Broken boundaries. That was what this was. And he was the one who'd done it.

*Idiot,* he chastised himself.

Surprise flickered in her gaze, but then her eyes turned molten. Reflecting what she must see in his.

'Shower first?' His voice was rough.

She agreed. Another broken boundary.

Jets of hot water spurted overhead as the two of them climbed into the large glass cubicle. He pulled her under the water, pressed her body against his and claimed her lips in a fierce kiss. He'd wanted to see how she would fit into his life, and now he knew. Wanted it despite himself. A life with Emma. A terrifying thought. He wanted it, but he could never have it.

'Thank you for being here,' he said, looking down into the depths of her eyes.

'I wouldn't be anywhere else, Alexander.'

Emma kissed him once more. Sensing that there was some sort of vicious battle raging inside him, she wanted to lighten the atmosphere. To take him back to having a good time and taking over the world. Carry his burden. That was why she was here. Because he needed her. What he didn't need was being needled for information. To talk about things he didn't want to.

With the water falling around them like rain, running down their bodies and pitter-pattering, on the tiled floor, Emma kissed a line down his torso as she went to her knees. His sky-blue eyes clouded over with lust, pupils dilating as he watched her lick his length.

Emma took him in her mouth and he groaned, low and deep. He was like steel encased in velvet in her hands. Teasing him with her tongue and her fingers and her warm, wet mouth, she watched him coming apart at the seams. One of his hands gently rested on the back of her head, the other was braced against the wet tiled wall as his hips began moving of their own accord.

Emma felt more alive than she ever had. Control and power ran through her veins, along with an arousal so strong it seared through her. *She* was making Alex come apart. This man that Aphrodite herself could have carved.

'Emma...' he said.

A breathless warning. One she wouldn't heed. Emma sucked deeper and his hips stilled, his body becoming rigid as he found his release. He pulled her up and kissed her thoroughly.

Laughter bubbled up, filling the space between them. Because *that* had been fun and overwhelming and consuming. Then, still breathing raggedly, and with a roguish smile, Alex returned the favour.

The breakfast that Alex had ordered was delivered soon after they got out of the shower, and Emma chose to finish her coffee out on the high-up balcony overlooking the river below. This apartment was so different from his other one. Just as luxurious. Filled with light and glass. But more masculine, with dark wood and brooding colours. The view was incredible too. There was no questioning which city she was in, with all the beautiful landmarks she could see.

'Penny for your thoughts?' Alex asked as he joined her.

Rain was starting to sprinkle overhead, and Emma tried her best to warm her hands on the coffee cup. Shivers racked her body.

'I was just thinking this place is so different from what I was expecting.'

He moved to stand behind her. Wrapping his arms around her waist. Drawing her into his warmth. 'And what was that?'

'A fancy high-tech townhouse in Mayfair or something.'

Alex laughed. 'I like being close to the water. And I can watch the boat race from up here.'

'The Regatta?' Emma asked.

'Mm-hmm.'

'Isn't rowing a bit slow for you?'

She couldn't imagine him doing anything that didn't involve wild amounts of speed. Rowing somehow seemed too tame a sport for Alex.

She knew he was rolling his eyes, even though she couldn't see it.

'I used to be on the team at university,' he said.

'That's impressive. It explains all the water-related art you have.'

'You noticed?'

Of course she had. There wasn't much Emma missed. Considering how she'd grown up, being observant had served her well. Noticing when to make herself scarce, when to give up something to Lauren, when to shield Maddison.

Alex tightened his hold on her. 'I sail now.'

'You do?'

'I have a sixty-footer.'

He pulled out his phone. She could hear him tapping the screen.

'Unfortunately, the weather is not ideal so we can't take her out.'

'That's okay.'

He frowned at the disappointment curdling in him. He didn't share his sailing with anyone apart from family and friends. But how wonderful it would have been to have her all to himself, with nothing but ocean around them, as he made her scream out his name over and over again.

'How long do I have you before I have to return you to the world?' Alex asked in a low voice, teeth nipping at her ear.

'Two weeks. I didn't know what I was walking into or how long you'd need me when I asked for leave,' she explained.

Two weeks. He liked the sound of that.

With rogue thoughts still clouding his usually sound

judgement, Alex decided they needed to get out. He'd take Emma on a tour of the city. Show her everything she would never have seen during past visits to London. It would be London as he knew it. No locked doors and even fewer rules.

They still had most of the two weeks ahead of them, and he resolved to enjoy it as much as possible.

He took her somewhere new each day.

That was when they weren't exploring each other in his bed or couch or kitchen.

They spent virtually every minute together.

It made them both forget, just for a little while, the end.

They visited Robert one more time, as promised, even though Alex video-called his father every day.

Buoyed by how much better he looked, they were at ease with leaving for Melbourne.

Alex's private jet stood on the tarmac, gleaming in the weak sunshine. He followed her up the stairs. Emma had grown up with money. There wasn't a thing on earth she couldn't buy. But this life that Alex led was on a different level. She didn't care to reflect on it. Not when Alex was leading her to one of the cream-coloured seats and buckling her in.

'You know, I'm perfectly capable of doing up my own belt.'

'I do know, but I'm enjoying getting to tie you down.'

She felt the colour rise up her neck as he ran his nose along her jaw, then seated himself across from her. She wondered what it would be like to be bound to his bed, with him having his way with her. Showing her pleasure as only he could. The look on his face told her that he had a direct line to her thoughts.

Once the plane had levelled off, a stewardess placed artful plates containing their lunch on the table between them. Throughout it, Emma kept casting longing glances at Alex, until she knew he couldn't take it any more.

Calling for two glasses of champagne, he handed one to Emma, then took her hand and led her to the bedroom at the back of the plane, where they crossed off another first…

Alex lay tangled in sheets that had damp patches on them, from where the champagne had run off Emma's body and collected in the fabric. With their chests heaving and sweat glistening on her skin, she drew abstract patterns on his hard torso, and he curled his arm under his head as he watched her fingers dance.

'Everything okay?' he asked, when at last she came down from her high and Emma was able to reply to the email that had pinged on her phone.

'Fiona wants a meeting as soon as I'm back. She says she wants to get going on things as quickly as possible.'

Emma propped her head up on her arm and looked down at Alex, who tucked the curtain of her hair behind her ear.

'She told me she wants to make the transition as smooth as possible and keep everyone on board. We're all volunteers anyway.'

Emma laughed to herself. A small sound that he knew held very little humour.

'I don't know how my family is going to react.'

'What are you going to tell them?'

'No idea. But I couldn't possibly disappoint them any more than I do already.'

She tried to cover up the sadness in her eyes, but he still saw it.

'Emma…' he whispered, and pulled her down into a kiss, wrapping his arms around her as her head came to rest on his chest. 'It hurts when your own blood doesn't acknowledge you, but you don't need them. They're just people. People who don't even really know you. Just be proud of yourself. You have achieved this without anyone.'

'That's not true. I've achieved this because of you, Alexander,' she said softly. 'I would never have met Fiona if it wasn't for you.'

'You would have found a way. I have no doubt.'

*Maybe*, she thought to herself.

But those words could have been said to him just as much as to her. It did hurt when family abandoned you. And no one would understand that more than Alex. A little boy abandoned first by his selfish mother and then by his father, when he chose to throw himself into his work.

She rested her chin on her hands as she turned to look at him. 'How do you do it?'

Strong fingers stroked through her hair. 'Do what?'

'Deal with it? Your mother was at that ball. I saw how angry you were. But you acted like she wasn't even there. Most of the time…' she tacked on at the end, remembering the look on his face when she had spoken to Emma.

'I told you. I don't have a mother.'

While his fingers still caressed her, and his arm still held her to him, his eyes wore that empty look that appeared whenever he shut his feelings away. A simple message. *Back off.* But Emma didn't want to. That woman had hurt him over and over again since he was a child.

'Except you do. She may not want to be, and you may not want her to be, but the fact is, she is.'

'Emma…' It was a warning.

'It's okay to be angry at her, Alexander. You're entitled to your feelings. But don't let that woman rule your life…destroy any happiness you could have in the future.'

Finally, those fingers stilled. He opened his mouth, but Emma cut him off before he could say anything unkind. She knew it would just be a defence mechanism. 'I'm not saying that happiness should be with me, or that you should find it any time soon. I'm just saying don't let her take away more from you than she already has. You're amazing, Alexander. You deserve more.'

She lifted her lips to his and kissed him. Kissed him until there was only heat scorching them. Until she felt weightless. Until the chill left his eyes. Until neither of them could breathe.

Alex rolled them over, lifted his head, and bathed her in that crooked smile that stopped her heart.

# CHAPTER EIGHTEEN

THE FIRST DAY back at work was torture. Emma could barely concentrate. London was still fresh in her mind. All she wanted was to be back there, in that apartment above the river. What they'd shared had been pure pleasure, and even her family's ire at her leaving for two weeks couldn't dampen her spirits. But it could make the day unbearably long.

Sitting in her office, Emma was taking a moment to gather her thoughts when there was a knock on the door.

'Fiona,' she said, getting to her feet, pleased that the morning had gone by. 'Please, take a seat.'

'Busy day?' Fiona asked as she sat down, elegantly crossing her legs.

'Like you wouldn't believe.' Emma looked at the closed glass door and the minimal privacy it provided. Everyone could see in, which meant her family would easily find out about Fiona's visit. 'Would you like to move to one of our meeting rooms?'

'Oh, there's no need. I'll be quick.'

Emma sat back in her chair. Butterflies had been unleashed in her stomach. Years of charity work had come to this point. She knew what Fiona wanted to talk about. Her small charity was finally going to soar as she'd always wanted it to. Excitement and trepidation in equal measure coursed through her.

'Everything is on track with the merger?' she asked.

'Yes, but that's not why I'm here.'

The serious look on Fiona's face had Emma's stomach plummeting. Had something gone wrong? Had her family interfered in some way? Did Fiona want the charity but not her? It wouldn't be the first time she hadn't been good enough, but she had done a great job so far. At least she thought so.

In the time it took Fiona to pull out a document from her bag, Emma considered every possibility that could have gone wrong. When Fiona slid the papers over, Emma had to make a gargantuan effort to keep from shaking.

'Relax, Emma,' Fiona said, clearly sensing her worry. 'Just take a moment to read this.'

Emma gave her a wary look but picked up the document. She read the top of the page and almost dropped it. Her eyes snapped to meet Fiona's.

'I'm not here for the charity, Emma. I'm here for you.'

The words *Offer of Employment* stared at her. Three times. She read it three times but still couldn't believe it. This was her dream.

'I thought you wanted to keep me on as a volunteer,' Emma finally managed to get out.

'I do. But you're too valuable an asset for me to overlook, Emma. You would be coming into a management role with us. I understand if this comes as a shock. After all, you do have other options.' Fiona looked around the small office. 'But, to be frank, I think you're wasted here.'

Emma scanned each line of the offer, falling more and more in love with the role. '*Do what makes you happy.*' That was what Alex had said. Heaven knew she wanted to. But, having been told over and over again since she was young what was expected of her, Emma didn't know how to do that when she was supposed to be here. In this tiny office. Until she was called upon.

'You don't have to decide immediately. Give it a day, think it over and then call me.' Fiona leaned forward in her chair, taking Emma's hand. 'There are many successful careers with us, Emma. I think this would only be the beginning for you.' Fiona stood and Emma followed her to the door. 'I really hope you say yes.'

'Thank you, Fiona.'

That was all Emma could manage. She watched her leave, then shut the door and dropped into her chair, reading through the offer again. This was what she had always wanted. Possibilities of a very different future ran through her mind then. Each one of them so much brighter than the path she was currently on.

She let herself imagine what it would be like. Not to have to be here every day. Not to feel like the spare daughter who wasn't wanted or needed. In front of her now was the opportunity to do something special. Words she wouldn't ever use to describe her job at Brown Hughs. Right now she was waiting. Waiting to be needed. Waiting for her life to start.

Emma wanted to make a difference. She knew she could do it. The only thing holding her back from immediately saying yes was her family. And, while she knew they wouldn't support her, she felt she owed them a chance to discuss her future. Or at the very least an explanation of why she wanted to leave.

The bravery to follow her dreams was what she needed now. Looking back on the past few weeks, she realised she had been braver than ever before. Exploring her sensuality with Alex, allowing him to see how her family affected her instead of always shoving the feelings away, letting him comfort her, flying to London to be with him. All those things had taken bravery.

Her phone was in her hand before she had even realised. Alex answered on the very first ring.

'Come out for a drink with me tonight? I have good news.'

'Where am I picking you up?' he asked, without even a moment's hesitation.

'My office.'

The floor was completely deserted. Emma's office was the only one occupied. If anyone walked by they would think that she was pulling long hours yet again. Nothing unusual.

Except she was obsessively rereading the offer.

'Stare any harder and you might set the paper on fire.'

She jumped at the voice and Alex laughed as he strode in. Heart leaping in her throat, she rose to step into his arms. His lips came down to meet hers in a gentle kiss that had her feeling giddy. Would she ever tire of this man?

'What's this good news?' he asked, keeping her pressed against his body.

Emma plucked the letter off the table and handed it to him. He stepped away from her, pacing as he read it. 'Tell me you've accepted.'

'Fiona told me to take a day to think it over.'

'You don't need one.'

Emma smiled. 'No, I don't.'

As conflicted as she felt, and having gone over every scenario a million times, there was one thing she kept coming back to: this was her dream. Surely she should be allowed to pursue that. There was nothing she did at Brown Hughs that someone else couldn't. No matter what happened after this, with her family or Alex, she would have one thing that made her truly happy.

The letter fell with a smack against the table as Alex dropped it, coming around her desk and yanking her to him. He kissed her hard and quick.

'This is the best news I've had all day. Let's go and celebrate,' he said, rubbing his nose along hers.

'Let's.'

Sipping the most delicious champagne she had ever tasted, in the most spectacular bar in Melbourne, Emma couldn't help but feel grateful for the man sitting beside her. Ever since she'd bumped into him her life had become so full. And now, as she stared out over her favourite city in the world, with Alex's lips on her neck and goosebumps racing along her arms, she understood that, despite her better judgement, she was irretrievably in love with him.

What a stupid, *stupid* thing to have let happen.

She wouldn't tell him. No. This was still a no-strings exploration of their off-the-charts chemistry. Nothing more.

'Do you want to go home?' he asked.

As if she was conditioned to respond instantly to him, Emma felt moisture pool in her core. The purr of his voice promised an unforgettable night.

'I want to go for a walk,' she said.

Telling him she loved him was off the table, but maybe she could share something of herself with him. Maybe he'd treasure it.

'Where are you taking me?' Alex asked.

'Somewhere special.' She smiled. 'My favourite place in the city. It may not seem like much to most, but I love it.'

Unlike the last time they'd walked through the streets and alleys, this time they couldn't bear not to touch. Alex laced his fingers in hers, holding tightly. It was such an innocent thing, holding hands. With them it didn't feel like it. It was the craving of having the other's skin on theirs. Feeling their heat and knowing they were one tug or pull away from losing all control.

If anyone had told Emma in the past that holding hands could feel like a sensual experience, she would have laughed at them. Now she knew the strength in those magic fingers. The safety of his touch. Felt the memories of each time he'd made her come apart.

'I'm going to tell my family tomorrow, after work,' she said, just to fill the silence that was burning through her so much that she'd almost given up on their walk altogether.

'Will you be okay?'

He looked down at her. Concern was what she saw in his eyes.

Emma shrugged her shoulders. 'I think so. Doesn't matter, though. It needs to be done. I'm following my dream, Alexander. Doing what makes me happy.'

'I'm glad to hear you say it.'

'Which means I can't see you.'

'Good thing we have tonight.'

'We're here,' Emma said in a quiet voice. 'This is it.'

Emma looked around her, feeling the same wonder she'd felt the first time she'd seen it.

They stood at an intersection, with buildings on all four corners. Glorious sand-coloured, weathered pieces of art. They stood golden in the streetlights. Their black, shadowed crevices only making them more breathtaking. And rising from each corner was a tall tree. Rough bark and smooth emerald leaves alike shared the golden illumination cast upon them.

'It's beautiful,' Alex said as he came up behind her, wrapping his arms around her waist. 'I can see why you like it so much.'

'I thought you would appreciate the Victorian architecture.'

'I do,' he said softly. 'Thank you for sharing this with me.'

Emma turned around in his arms. 'Thank you for appreciating it.'

She felt the apprehension leaving her body as he drew her to him, his gaze pulling her in. He took her face in his hands and pressed his lips to hers. Long and slow. Tongues entwining. Drowning in each other. It was a miracle they were still on their feet. She had never felt such a primal need to be with someone as she did right now.

He was like a beacon in the darkness. She could kiss him forever. She wanted to. And the fact that he was kissing her here, in her favourite place, broke and mended and shattered something within her.

# CHAPTER NINETEEN

ALEX SAT IN his office. He had a morning of back-to-back meetings and a slew of issues that he'd normally tackle head-on. Not today. He was distracted. In fact, he'd cut the last meeting short because he hadn't been able to handle being in that room when his every thought was of Emma.

Last night, he'd thought that a day apart from her was exactly what he needed. He'd felt so off balance since they had returned. Emma was starting to make him question why he lived his life the way he did. The way he always had. It was something he wasn't willing to accept. He'd thought a tiny bit of space would do them both a world of good, even as his chest had tightened at the prospect. As if his body had physically rejected the idea.

When had he ever worried about anyone like this? Or at all? Somehow she had found a way under his skin and he cared now. More than he should. Because he still intended to walk away.

Convincing himself that leaving had always been the best course of action, Alex figured that when the time came, walking away would be the greatest show of his caring. There was no happy future with him.

Emma needed someone capable of love. Not someone who hadn't been good enough for a mother who had abandoned him or a father who had left him to his loneliness. That same blood flowed through his veins, and he was damned if he would ever do that to anyone. Or allow them to do it to him. When their attraction was gone, Emma would leave, and he wasn't going to risk becoming like his father, no matter how brilliant the man was.

His thoughts didn't stop him from picking up the phone and calling her. When she answered, her voice was like a warm caress over his skin.

'Alexander.'

'Ripped off the Band-Aid yet?'

Her musical laugh came through, wrapping around his spine with a tingle.

'Not yet. I was just about to call my mother.'

'Good luck.' Alex paused. He wanted to offer to be there with her. Protect her. But he knew it wasn't his place.

'Emma…'

'Alex…'

They spoke at the same time and laughed.

'You first,' he said.

'Thank you for checking in,' Emma said.

Alex held the phone to his ear, picturing what she looked like now and how she would feel later. 'Remember why you're doing this,' he said.

'I will.'

She sighed, and he had the strangest feeling she was trying not to say something.

'I'll talk to you later.'

Emma placed her phone on the table. She had been putting off calling her mother all day, but speaking to Alex had given her the little shove she needed.

Lifting the receiver of her desk phone, Emma called her mother's extension. 'Hi, Mom, I need a favour.'

'What is it, Emma?' Helen Brown's distracted voice came through.

'I need to talk to all of you tonight. Do you think you can make that happen?' Emma asked. Her heart was pounding in her chest.

'Sure, darling. Shall we have a family dinner? Is Alex coming?'

Family dinners were torture. The thought of having to sit through a meal after she gave them the news was too much to bear. Maybe if she spoke to them after the meal? That was sure to be unpleasant, and there was no way they would allow her to make them wait when she had called for everyone to be present.

'No. I won't be long, and Alex is working.'

'Okay. What time will you come over?'

'Straight after work. Six?'

'That's fine. See you later, Em.'

Emma hung up and scrunched her fingers in her hair. It was ridiculous that she should feel scared. This was her flesh and blood. They had raised her. For better or worse, they would be in her life forever.

The problem was she was certain tonight would be for worse...

\* \* \*

Emma drove through the city and eventually came to the tree-lined roads of Toorak. The houses were as big as the bank accounts around here, and that was exactly what her family liked.

She pulled up to the gates of her family home and pressed the button on the little remote that lived in her car. She waited for the gates to swing open and then rolled the car to a spot on the driveway where she always parked when she wanted a quick exit.

Emma eyed the behemoth of a house, with its towering walls and smooth pillars. It was a stately mansion, and ordinarily she would have appreciated it. Except she had grown up within its walls, and there was nothing she coveted more than the small sanctuary she now called home.

Emma took a deep breath at the front door. Her palms were already sweaty. She straightened her dress and walked in.

'Mom?' she called.

A round table stood in the middle of the hall, with an obnoxiously large flower arrangement in its centre. Two sweeping staircases clung to the wall, beckoning her in as if the house itself offered a welcoming hug. But even shiny polished banisters couldn't help the cold that lived within.

'Emma?' Her mother's head poked out from the doorway.

'Hi, Mom.' Emma hugged her mother.

'You look nervous. Everything okay?'

Emma nodded.

'Okay, well…everyone's here.'

Her mother walked back the way she'd come and Emma followed her into the dining room, where everyone had taken their usual seats. Emma decided sitting was probably better than standing. It wouldn't seem as if she was impatient to flee, even though she was.

'What's this about, Emma?' asked her father as she took her seat at the opposite end of the table. As far as possible from him.

*You can do this,* she told herself.

'I have an announcement to make, and I want to tell you all in person—not drop a surprise on you at the office.'

It was the truth. If there was a scene to be made, she would rather they dealt with it in private than have an audience. No doubt that would cause all sorts of rumours to spread like wildfire throughout the company, the way gossip often did. She didn't want that for Brown Hughs.

Lauren narrowed her eyes. 'Have you done something?'

Emma smiled. A full, beaming, megawatt smile. 'Yes, something good. As you all know, a few years back I joined a small literacy charity as a volunteer.'

'Ugh, that charity again?' Lauren scoffed.

'Yes, the charity, Lauren.' Emma forced herself to remain calm. She wasn't going to get upset or angry. It wouldn't help her. 'Recently I've had a few meetings with a large national charity, and they were so impressed with us that they've decided to merge our organisation into theirs.'

'That's wonderful news, honey,' said her mother.

'It is. Now we'll be well funded, and we can reach so many more people. But that's not why I'm here.' Emma took a deep breath. 'I have been offered a management position in the organisation and I've decided to accept.'

She looked at everyone, waiting for the explosion. They were all silent.

Maddison was the first to show any response at all. She grabbed Emma's hands with her own, a broad smile on her face. 'You're going to be amazing!' she said, elated.

Their mother, on the other hand, looked worried. But the sight that really burst her bubble was the delighted sneer on Lauren's face and her father turning what could only be called puce.

'Charity!'

Emma froze in shock. It had been years since she'd been yelled at by her father, and of all the reactions she'd thought of, this wasn't one of them.

'Do I need to remind you of who you are, Emma? Being a Brown means you have a responsibility. Each one of us has to grow this family's standing and our wealth for the next generation—and you want to abandon that duty?'

Emma's hands curled into fists. 'Abandon my duty?' Her voice rose, but she didn't care that she was addressing her father. 'How could anything increase a family's standing more than doing charity work, Dad? And I didn't say I was leaving the company tomorrow. I'm prepared to do what's expected of me. I always have been. But what's the point of me sitting in that shoebox of an office with all the potential I have and doing nothing with it? You won't even give me a chance.'

'Your *potential*?' he said scornfully.

'Peter. That's enough,' her mother said firmly, and for once he listened. 'Emma, I'm so proud of you for following your dreams, sweetheart, but this isn't the most appropriate path for you.'

'Why not?' Emma was struggling to get her words out now. She refused to cry in front of her family. Her throat burned from unshed tears.

'Because we're not people who can do as we please,' said Lauren. 'There are expectations of us. That's how we got to where we are. You can't walk around with your head in the clouds.'

Their father clapped her on the shoulder. Such a blatant show of where his approval lay. And Lauren's smug expression was clear to everyone.

Emma shook her head. One person. Only one person at this table was happy for her. But there wouldn't be a thing Maddison could say that the others would listen to.

Hurt beyond words, Emma stood up. 'I wanted to tell you, and I have.' Emma placed a folded glossy brochure on the table, so her family could see what she had managed to make happen. 'I'll see you at work,' she croaked.

She turned to go but her father stopped her.

'If you go ahead with this, that's it. You will be cut off,' he said.

Emma spun around. 'Would you like me to pay back my trust fund as well?' she spat.

Helen bolted between father and daughter. 'Peter.

Emma. Stop it. That money was to set you up for life and we wouldn't ever take it back.'

'Of course you *would* defend her!' Peter shouted at his wife. 'She was a mistake from the beginning, and now she's an accident that is costing us, and it's your fault.' He turned his cold hazel gaze to Emma. 'You do this and you are no longer my daughter.'

Emma staggered back at his words. It was like a dagger plunged into her chest. Even Lauren had the good grace to look shocked.

'Was I ever?' she asked in a small voice.

'You can cut her off, Peter, but I will not have you attack my daughter like that,' her mother fired at her husband. 'Emma—'

She went to hug her daughter, but Emma recoiled from her touch. With one last look at everyone, she fled.

# CHAPTER TWENTY

EMMA RAN TO her car and started it up in a daze. She drove away from the large house completely numb. As if she was completely detached from her body. She barely noticed the rain starting to fall, or the roads she took. Not even the numbers she pressed to gain access to the car park in Alex's building.

It was only when she was at his door that she realised where it was she had driven to. She stared at the key in her hand. The key Alex hadn't taken back. She was breaking, and he would make her feel whole again. But then what?

Right now, she didn't care. Emma just wanted to feel.

She slid the key into the lock and pushed at the large swivel door. The apartment was bathed in bright golden light. Soft music floated overhead, drowning out the raindrops battering the windows. She closed the door behind her, and with the sound of her heels and the snap of the door she knew Alex would have heard her enter.

He walked out with a folder in his hand that he dropped to the table the instant he saw her, and the numbness ebbed away, only to be replaced by a torrent of emotions washing over her. It was overwhelming.

Alex took one look at her face and she knew he'd see that it had gone badly with her family.

Closing the distance between them, he pulled her into a protective hug. 'Do you want to talk about it?' he asked.

Did she? Part of her did. Part of her wanted to wail. But maybe forgetting would be better.

And as she sorted through all the thoughts occurring to her at once, the only thing she was certain of was that she didn't want to let go of him just yet. So she stayed in his arms.

'What's that?' she asked, staring at the manila folder on the table.

It wasn't work, because she had come to learn that everything in his office had the company logo. Every document was logged.

Still keeping his arms around her, he pulled back to see what she was looking at. 'The results from my yearly medical check-up.'

'Healthy as a horse?' she teased. But her voice wasn't bright or cheery.

'Yeah, all clear. I wasn't expecting you tonight,' he said.

She didn't respond. It was true—so what was she doing here? She should have gone home to Hannah and Lucky.

'I know.' A heavy sigh escaped her lips. 'I should go.'

Emma huffed a laugh, feeling a little silly. This wasn't a normal relationship. It had never been. And she had fully expected her family to react badly. She'd been prepared for that.

Alex frowned. 'Come with me.'

He led her to the one place in his home that he knew made her happy. From the moment he'd shown it to her Emma had felt that the library was a safe space. She would often curl up on the couch with whatever book she was reading whenever he had to take a call he just couldn't ignore.

Pulling her down to the couch, Alex draped her legs over his. 'Talk to me, Emma.'

Blinking away tears, she bit her lip. Still not feeling entirely composed, somehow she managed to tell him exactly what had happened when she went to her parents' home. As she spoke, Alex's eyes became more and more glacial.

'I'm sorry, Emma. But you don't need them. You don't need their approval. You're nothing like them.'

'It still hurts.'

'I know it does.'

Alex ran his hand up her arm and over her shoulder, caressing her neck with a protective touch. Her hand came to rest on his cheek. Fingertips stroking the stubble she found there. She kissed his jaw, shifting so his lips could come down to hers. It was the softest brush. He was watching her, waiting for a sign of what she needed, but he didn't have to wait.

Emma closed her eyes and leaned in, wanting more. Opening up for him. He sucked her bottom lip into his mouth and her hand moved to the back of his neck, pulling him closer. His scent wrapped around her and she got exactly what she wanted. His tongue dancing with hers, growing the need between them. Heat building within her. A heat that she could focus on. That would distract her from the swirling thoughts of inadequacy.

And then her lips were urgent on his. Desperate. As if he was a life raft she was clinging to. His arms locked so tightly around her that he might as well have been. And then her lips were gone from his. Kissing his sharp jaw, his strong neck.

Alex cursed. 'Emma,' he said, in a rough, strangled way. 'I'm out of protection.'

She wasn't meant to come over tonight after all.

Emma pulled away to look into his eyes, which were darkened with need. 'I don't care. I want you, Alexander.'

Cradling her head in his large hands, he gazed at her intensely. 'Are you sure?'

'Yes. I promise.'

'I trust you,' he said, and kissed her once more.

Picking her up bridal-style, Alex carried her to his bedroom and laid her down on the king-size bed. Holding himself up over her, he kissed her softly.

'I'm going to ask you again. Are you sure about this?' Alex whispered.

'Yes,' she replied, wanting him heart and soul, and in that very moment she couldn't think of anything else.

His fingers went to the ties on her blue wrap dress. Pulled on it slowly. It unravelled, the fabric falling away slightly. His lips moved to the exposed skin of her side while his hands pushed the rest of the fabric away. Trailing open-mouthed kisses across her stomach to her hip, and then up her body and over her shoulder, he peeled the dress away. She never took her eyes off him.

Alex helped her out of her dress and tossed it aside.

Her bra was next.

He sucked her clavicle, teeth nipping at her earlobe.

'You're so damn beautiful,' Alex said on a breath, and her heart stuttered.

He kissed her neck.

'Intelligent…'

He sucked her nipple into his mouth and drew a moan from deep within her.

'Kind…'

A kiss above her belly button.

'Determined…'

His mouth came to her sex. He traced his tongue slowly through her slickness.

'Perfect.'

'Alexander…'

It was part moan, part sob. He wanted to hear her say it again. It made him feel like Icarus, flying too close to the sun. And she had become the sun. The centre of his world.

With his tongue and his hands, he worshipped her. He was focused on her. On being in this moment. On getting to love her in this intimate way that slightly terrified him—because what if he could never let go after tonight?

Her fingers sank into his hair as her hips bucked beneath him, but he didn't slow down. He kept going until his name was an incantation on her lips as she came apart. Waves of pleasure rolling through her.

The apartment became silent.

Emma's eyes were tightly shut, her chest rising and falling rapidly. He kissed her everywhere. Along her thighs, over her belly, on her neck. Until she caught her breath. Then Alex could wait no more.

He pulled away, standing at the foot of the bed. Grasping the front of his shirt, he ripped it in opposite directions, sending buttons popping off and clattering to the floor in a shower. He divested himself of the rest of his clothes and then he was hovering over her, holding himself up on his arms.

Their gazes locked together. Alex leaned his forehead on Emma's and slowly sank into her. His moan was guttural. Being careful, disciplined, was who Alex was, so he had never done this before. What they had was so powerful, what was one more first between them?

'You feel amazing...'

Alex had never felt this connected to a soul in his life. He wanted to savour every moment of the feeling. He took his time. Moving slowly, languorously.

He was always in control, but she was making him lose it. Dissolving all the strings that kept him so rigidly in place. Making him question why he'd ever thought he could live without this. This wasn't sex. It wasn't fun. It was love. And he was drowning in it.

Alex could feel Emma climbing. She was bearing down on him. Her gasps coming in quick, almost musical pants. And then her body arched and she shattered around him, moaning incoherently. Unable to breathe and completely overwhelmed.

Alex kissed her hard as he rode her through her release and into his own as it crashed into him. His moan was quiet. Ragged. Vulnerable. Their lips were still connected. He pushed all the way into her silken depths, unable to disconnect himself from her.

Looking down at Emma, he saw tears run down the sides of her face. He brushed them away but said nothing.

Because he felt it too.

They had been irrevocably changed.

# CHAPTER TWENTY-ONE

THE SKY WAS only just lightening to a deep blue when Emma woke. After a few sleepy blinks she felt her brain catch up, and remembered the events of the night before. Every night with Alex was great, but last night had been soul-consuming. She knew he'd felt what she had—it had been clear in his eyes.

So when she looked over and saw that his side of the bed was empty, she got an uneasy feeling in the pit of her stomach. He had woken up with her every day they'd spent in London. In that little fantasy bubble.

Emma dressed hurriedly in the clothes she'd worn the day before. She would have to leave soon, if she had any chance of going home to change and still getting to work on time. Not that she was keen to. The confrontation with her family was still fresh in her mind.

She found her shoes in the library and slipped them on before rushing downstairs, where she found Alex.

'There you are.'

He placed a mug of coffee on the counter for her and she took a grateful sip before kissing him. It didn't feel right.

Emma gathered her things. There was a message from Hannah on her phone.

Lucky is fed. Heading out early.

Emma chuckled at her phone. Her cat would no doubt be upset that she had spent another night away. But it was nothing he wouldn't forgive with a few tasty treats.

She noticed Alex was being unusually quiet.

'Alexander? Are you okay?' she asked, holding the mug in her hand.

'Of course. Why?'

'Well, you've only said three words to me. Usually…'

Usually he wouldn't be able to keep his hands off her.

Usually he had a flirty smile for her, or a naughty wink.

'Emma.'

She didn't like his tone.

'Can we talk before I leave for work?'

'What do you want to talk about?' he asked. She could smell his tea from the other side of the counter.

'Last night was…' Words failed him.

'Yes, it was,' she said quietly.

She looked up and he was studying her. She held his gaze until he walked around the kitchen counter and stood before her. Putting her cup down, she took his hands in hers.

'Alexander, you pieced me back together last night.'

He caressed her cheek, but he looked so composed. Too composed. 'You should never have been broken in the first place,' he said.

Emma shrugged. The feeling that something was amiss just would not leave her. 'What's wrong?' she insisted.

'Nothing,' he said forcefully.

'Really? Because for the first time since I met you I don't believe you,' she said testily, brushing his hand away.

'I don't know what to tell you, Emma...'

She shook her head, anger quickly heating her blood. 'I don't believe this. We have a real connection, and your next move is to shut me out.'

'I'm not shutting you out.'

'What do you call this? What you're doing right now?' She took a breath, and turned around to get her coat, but he caught her wrist, drawing her back.

'I told you from the beginning that I can't change. I was honest with you. And I was honest with you last night.'

'But you're not being honest this morning. I didn't ask you to change. Not once. Not...'

Emma had opened her mouth to yell at him, but she stopped. Instead, she closed her eyes and took a deep breath, and when she opened them she was calm. The shutters had come down on her feelings. She knew she was falling into the abyss now, but no one would see.

It made Alex snap. 'For God's sake, Emma, stop doing that! Feel what you feel! If you're angry, show me, dammit!'

It was the most out-of-control she had ever seen him.

'Not when you became the most important person to me. Not when I fell in love with you,' she said softly.

Her eyes welled up. She was damned if she would let the tears fall. 'I love you, Alexander.'

She loved him.

She watched the words fall on him like a blade. All he could do was shake his head.

'I don't do love, Emma! I don't know how to.'

There was desperation and agony and no small amount of sorrow on his face.

She stepped closer and cupped his cheek. 'It breaks my heart that you think that. Because you love harder than anyone I know. Maybe one day you'll figure it out.'

Alex dropped his head and pulled her hand away from his face. 'Emma, I can't change—even if I want the same things. You're better off with someone else,' he said.

'Goodbye, Alex.'

She placed his apartment key on the counter, picked up her things and left. Her heart breaking. This was never meant to last. And she knew she would never love again. Not like this.

She felt as if she had to fight for every breath. She had always known this day would come, and yet she still felt woefully unprepared. Climbing into her car, she slammed her head against the headrest, fighting the tears that she didn't want to shed.

'Keep it together!' she told herself.

Her phone sprang into life, Alex's face flashing on the caller ID. But she rejected the call and threw her phone onto the passenger seat. There was nothing he could say now. She knew what they'd shared. What he wasn't ready for.

The car tore out of the parking bay and she rushed home. Not even once glancing back at his building. She was a vortex of grief and anger. Within the course of one night she had lost the one bright light in her life and lost most of her family. And neither because she had done anything wrong.

It didn't matter. Emma felt resolved. She knew what she had to do.

Hannah had already left when Emma arrived home. Lucky, her beautiful black cat, had a full bowl of food and obstinately ignored her, angry that she hadn't been home. She pulled out a couple of his favourite treats, bribing him for his forgiveness, before she readied herself for work and rushed out through the door.

Emma clocked in with minutes to spare. Normally the friendliest person on the floor, this morning she barely greeted anyone. Everyone who saw her simply moved aside to let her pass. She was immediately reminded of Alex, and she felt as if she was suffocating.

She shut the door to her office with a rattle. She was done. Done with all the people in her life, done with this company, done with living in hope.

Her laptop was fired up and she typed a resignation letter, printed it in her office. The next thing she did was save all her personal files on a thumb drive and wipe them from the hard drive. There wasn't much, but it felt final.

She knew the correct protocol was to hand her resignation letter to her manager, but she was a Brown, and she wanted to look at the glee on her father's face when she gave it to him.

Snatching up the letter, she took the elevator up to the executive floor and barged into her father's office. She didn't even acknowledge her mother or Lauren, who were with him.

Her father opened his mouth to yell at her. Not willing to give him the opportunity to say anything, she slapped her letter down on the table.

'What's this?' he asked, irritated by her interruption.

'I'm leaving, if you recall,' Emma said. Her voice was hard. 'But I will work out my notice period.'

His eyes scanned the page. 'If you want to leave, you should go.'

'Are you firing me?' she asked in a steely tone.

Her father stared her down, but for once, Emma was not moved. She stood straighter. Unintimidated.

'Dad, are you firing me?' she repeated.

'Yes.'

'Peter!' her mother exclaimed.

'Fine.'

It was exactly the outcome she'd wanted. It wasn't about the pay-out she'd receive—rather that everyone would know that Peter Brown had fired his hardest working daughter, and she silently wished him luck in sorting that mess out.

Initially she'd wanted to save the image of the company. Now she didn't care. Now she would be able to walk into her dream job without having to wait.

Emma was almost through the door when she turned around. There was something she had to get off her chest.

'I know you don't approve of my passion for charity work, and you don't have to, but just know that I was the one who ignored every dream to be what this company needed, and now I'm doing this for me. I don't need you.'

She closed the door behind her and went back down to her office to gather her things. Glad that she wasn't the sentimental type, and there wasn't much to take apart from the framed degree that hung behind her. Placing it carefully on the desk, Emma looked around at the tiny office and realised that, as much as she'd enjoyed working with the people here, she would not miss the place.

A knock at the door made her jump and spin around to see Greg in the doorway.

'Can I see you in my office?' he asked.

Emma picked up her framed degree and her bag, and without a backward glance followed her manager who gestured for her to take a seat in front of his desk.

He sat heavily in his chair. 'Where do we start, Emma? I can't believe you were fired.'

She lifted her shoulders nonchalantly, an action completely at odds with how she felt inside. 'It was going to happen sooner or later.'

'I know. But it's unbelievable. I just want you to know it's been a pleasure to work with you and you'll always have friends here.'

'Thank you, Greg.'

'And if there's ever anything you need, just call.'

She gave him a hug, and had to fight tears she hadn't expected from leaving Brown Hughs. Then she picked up her belongings and headed out to her car.

She idly wondered how long it would be before her name was removed from her parking space. Driving out, she glimpsed the handyman in her mirror. He was walking to her spot and she knew.

A song wafted through the speakers in her car as she joined the road but Emma turned it off. She couldn't bear any more music. Her heart couldn't take it. There were too many good memories of Alex. And one soul-crushing one. She felt like an idiot for ever thinking she could hold on to those memories when the last memory tainted all the others.

Her phone rang again. This time it was Hannah. She pressed a little button on her steering wheel and her best friend's voice came through loudly in the car.

'How are you holding up, Em? I heard.'

'That was quick. How?'

'Maddison called me. She sounded genuinely concerned,' said Hannah's disembodied voice. 'She said your dad said some harsh things.'

No doubt Lauren would have filled Maddison in the moment Emma was out the door. 'I don't really know what to say,' she told Hannah.

'That makes two of us. And I can tell that's not the only thing. What's going on?'

Emma huffed a laugh. Of course Hannah would be perceptive. She knew Emma better than anyone.

'Emma?'

'Alex and I broke up.'

And they were the words that broke the dam.

'Oh, Em, I'm so sorry! I can take the rest of the day off?' Hannah offered.

'No. I just want to be alone.'

There was nothing anyone could say or do that would help her now. She knew that what she and Alex had shared was temporary. He'd always been honest with her. Emotions didn't follow logic, though, and she felt as if there was a rip right through her soul.

'I understand. Call me if you need anything. Okay? Anything.'

'Thanks, Han. I'll see you later.'

Emma hung up just as she reached her building. With heavy steps, she made her way up to her apartment. Lucky was still ignoring her. She dropped her things on the small dining table and flopped onto the couch, where she curled up and let the tears fall. With arms wrapped around herself she sobbed, feeling completely bereft.

Lucky jumped off his perch and pounced on the cushions, pushing his way between her arms. She scratched his head, but nothing could stem the flow.

# CHAPTER TWENTY-TWO

'GOODBYE, ALEX.'

*Alex*. That had crushed him.

All he'd been able to do was watch her leave and feel a part of him fracture.

He'd felt like raging. He'd wanted to break something. Tear his apartment apart. But he'd done none of that. He'd controlled his shattering heart, standing inhumanly still.

He'd stood rooted to the spot as he'd heard the door close behind her. The silence had been deafening. All he'd been able to feel was his lungs expanding and contracting. Everything else had fallen away. He was hollow.

'What did I just do?' he asked himself now.

A voice at the back of his mind told him it was the right thing, but it didn't feel like it. He was sure Emma hated him now, and that felt worse than any torture he could imagine. Hadn't he wondered what a life with her would be like? Except he'd told her to find someone else. He didn't want to picture that. It hurt beyond words.

He'd called her, wanting to apologise, to ask her back, but his call had been rejected.

He ran his fingers through his hair, as if somehow that was going to fix all the broken pieces inside him. It did make him move. Back to his room, where he looked at the bed. His cruel mind replayed images of Emma stretched out over it, calling his name. Of him watching her sleep last night after she'd toppled his world.

Alex backed away from the piece of furniture as if it were a dangerous animal. He showered and dressed robotically. What he needed was work. Something to stop him feeling as if the walls were crumbling.

He walked into his study and was assaulted by the memory of kissing Emma against the door. A heavy sigh escaped him. She was going to haunt him.

Sending a message to the office to say that he would be working from home, Alex sat at his desk and forced himself to concentrate. He ignored the beauty of the sunrise outside his window. He ignored every intruding thought of her. Even though he knew ignoring everything around him wasn't going to fix the gnawing void within.

No music played this morning. When he was younger, music had filled the stifling silence. Being an only child, with no mother and a father lost to his grief, had made for a silent childhood. Emma had said it sounded lonely. She had no idea. Music had made the space feel less empty, and as he'd matured he had grown so used to it that it had become one of those things he didn't think about. Just the norm.

Now he couldn't bear the thought of it. Any music would just set his teeth on edge.

For a few hours he worked through the list of tasks he had set for himself, but the ringing of the phone on his laptop brought that to a halt. He accepted the call, and Matt's concerned face filled his screen.

'Are you okay?' Matt asked.

'How did you…?'

'Hannah just told me. What happened, mate?'

And Alex told him the edited version of events.

'Alex, I could punch you right now.'

'I know I hurt her,' Alex said.

'You didn't just hurt her, mate. When are you going to see that you're punishing yourself for a mistake that wasn't even yours? You know you love her. I saw it. I'm sure everyone else did too!'

Alex saw Matt look away, his eyes unfocussed, as if he was deep in thought. 'You keep saying that you can't change, but you're lying to yourself.'

'I'm not ready for that, Matt.'

'That's another lie. You're gutted, mate. It's not too late. You can fix this.'

'I don't think I can,' Alex said, propping his elbows on the table and running his hands over his face.

'I've known you for ever, Alex. I don't believe that for a second. You deserve to be happy, mate.'

Alex appreciated the words. He just didn't know if he could believe them just yet.

Matt ended the call and Alex stared at the ceiling, wondering if he'd done the right thing.

By the time the evening came round, he felt more

like a shell than ever. He poured a measure of whisky into a cut-glass tumbler and sought the sanctuary of his library. Yes, it would remind him of Emma, but it was also the room with the best distractions.

When Alex entered the room, he knew exactly which book he wanted, but the one on the table was what caught his eye. It was Emma's favourite. His favourite. He picked it up and lifted the cover. Her bookmark fell out.

Snapping it shut, he raised his arm to hurl it across the room, but couldn't. Instead, he sank into a plush chair and started reading.

He felt as if his heart was tearing itself apart and then stitching itself together and tearing apart again, like some sort of Promethean torment. And he felt as if he deserved an eternity of it.


Lucky sat at Emma's bedroom door and, as usual, she picked him up and took him to her bed, where he curled up on the pillow next to hers. Emma was restless. Her family were silent. The person she wanted was an impossibility. Hannah was working late. There was only one person she could call.

The phone rang for an age before her mother answered. 'Emma?'

'Hey, Mom,' she greeted her as she climbed under the covers.

'How are you, sweetheart?'

'I'm okay,' she said tiredly.

Emma wanted to tell her mother everything. She

wanted her to come over and hug her and tell her it would be okay. That she was wrong and would love again.

'Darling, is this important? I'd love to chat, but Maddie is here,' her mother said.

Pure mirthless laughter bubbled up in Emma's throat. She choked it down. Why had she thought she would find solace in her parent? She wasn't Maddie or Lauren. Her mother might have tried to defend her to her father, but that didn't seem to mean all that much. Alex had been right about one thing: she didn't need them.

'No, Mom, don't worry about it. I'll talk to you later.' Emma hung up before her mother could say anything more. 'Well, Lucky,' she said, turning over to face her cat. 'Looks like it's just you and I.'

The black cat chirped and continued licking his paws while Emma watched. At least she had one love that would never leave her...

# CHAPTER TWENTY-THREE

WHEN ALEX SAW his father's name flash on his phone, he was instantly filled with guilt. He hadn't called to make sure his father was okay for two days. Hadn't checked on his progress.

'What's happened, son?' his father asked.

'Nothing. I'm sorry I haven't called.' He looked at the time and realised how late it was in the UK. 'You should be asleep, Dad. You know what the cardiologist said.'

'Alex, I feel fine. My recovery is going well, and it was just a minor heart attack. Now, tell me what's happened, so your old man doesn't stress.'

Alex sighed and looked away, debating what he should tell his father. When he was growing up, it had seemed as if the man had always known when he was hiding something. Alex had quickly learned to tell the whole truth and own up to his actions. If he didn't tell his father what was wrong, he had no doubt he would figure it out anyway.

So he told him everything. Even what he'd left out with Matt.

He didn't know why he was letting everything out

like this—he never shared emotional stuff with anyone. He was stronger than that. But it all poured out of him and he knew he couldn't stop it if he tried.

'Son, you are not me, and Emma is not Catherine,' his father told him when Alex stopped talking. 'You love each other in a way we never did. At times I was a little too domineering, but that isn't who you are. Emma isn't going to leave you a broken man, like I was when your mother left. You're broken because you left her.'

'Dad—' Alex started, but a look from his father made him stop.

'That's what you are afraid of and that's what's made you run now. She's the only person you've dated that you've brought home.'

'She's the only person I've actually dated, Dad.' He had had encounters in the past. Purely physical releases. Emma had been different from the very beginning.

His father shut his eyes tightly. 'That's my fault,' he said sadly.

'What do you mean?' Alex frowned. He'd never blamed his father. He was his hero. Just as much a victim of his mother as he had been until he'd decided he wouldn't be.

'Over the years, every time you asked about your mother and didn't get the answers you wanted, you retreated into yourself a little more. I didn't know how to handle it. I was so caught up in my own loss. I really did love your mother, but I didn't show it. And then it was too late.'

'It was too late because you wanted an heir,' Alex said simply.

'No, Alex, I wanted a child. I didn't care about the title; my brother could have had it. Maybe then you would have had cousins. It doesn't change the fact that I should have been there for you. You would have been so much happier. But I wasn't, and I'm sorry.'

Alex's lips pressed into a thin line. 'Dad, you were there. You were the only one who was.'

Robert shook his head. 'Not enough. But I will tell you now what I should have then. Your mother leaving was not your fault, son. And it wasn't mine either. It was her own decision. She wasn't capable of giving you the love you needed.'

Alex felt something inside him crumble. 'Dad…' He barely got the word out.

'I'm proud of the man you've become, Alex, and that man doesn't run when it gets tough.'

'But I did.' Alex dropped his gaze and said softly, 'I miss her.'

'Then get her back. She makes you happy, son, and that's all a parent ever wants for their child.'

Alex pinched the bridge of his nose. As usual, his father was right. But he was scared. And that was hard to admit to himself.

'Go, son. Don't waste any more time.'

Alex listened. He hung up and shoved his phone in his pocket, then slipped on the jacket of his blue three-piece suit. Picking up his keys, he hurried to his car and rushed over to Brown Hughs. When he arrived at her office with a racing heart he found it empty. There was no sign of her. Not even her degree on the wall.

He went to the office of her manager, who was walking around his desk, going back to his chair.

'Where's Emma?' Alex asked.

'You don't know?' Greg's brow furrowed.

'Know what?' Alex growled.

'You should speak to her family.' He threw the file he was holding onto the table, clearly upset.

Alex was already on the move. He had no idea how they could have made life any worse for her, but being on edge and emotional had his temper simmering just below the surface.

The elevator doors slid open on the C Suite floor, and as luck would have it he ran into Lauren.

'Alex!' she said, surprised.

'Where's your father?'

His tone was sharp and low. Lauren clearly recognised the edge in it and had him follow her to her father's office. She walked in behind Alex and silently closed the door.

'Alexander Hastings!'

Peter Brown greeted him warmly, but his eyes were cold. Cruel.

'This is a surprise. How can I help you?'

'Where's Emma?' Alex stared the man down. He was not in the mood for pretences.

'As of two days ago she no longer works here,' Peter said.

'What did you do?' Alex clenched his fists at his sides.

'What did *I* do? You dare barge into my office and question *me*?' Peter was incensed. 'I fired her, and it was about time too. I don't have time for anyone who abandons their duty to their family for frivolous pursuits.'

Alex had to fight every urge to punch the man in front of him. 'You fired your daughter?' he said slowly. Disbelief turning into blazing fury.

Helen rushed into the office. Out the corner of his eye, Alex saw her enter, but he didn't acknowledge her. Not even when she called his name.

'It's none of your business,' Peter spat.

Alex brought his palms down onto the glossy wooden desk, leaning over this man he hated with a passion. 'Oh, it's very much my business. Every time you hurt Emma, it's my business,' Alex snarled, his pulse pounding in his ears. 'Let me tell you right now, if by some miracle she ever lets you back into her life, and you cause her even the slightest bit of distress, I will have no problem coming after you with everything I've got. You've been warned.'

'You think you can threaten m—?' Seeing the look in Alex's eyes, Peter let the words die on his tongue.

Alex brushed past the two women. He had had enough of the Browns for one day. All he wanted was to find Emma.

'She's at home.'

It was the last thing he heard. He didn't thank Helen.

Emma had her feet curled up on the couch. Lucky lay against her, happily dozing, while Emma watched whatever was on the flatscreen TV. She didn't care. She felt empty. Grief-stricken. There was plenty to mourn—her job, her family, a relationship that had been doomed from the start.

The laptop she'd been working on stood open on the coffee table. Words she couldn't concentrate on stared back at her. Judging her. She'd allowed herself these two days. A lot had happened, but tomorrow would be the start of a new journey. A new Emma. The Emma she was some of the time. Except now she could be her all of the time. She no longer had a family who could make her feel as if she needed to withdraw. Tomorrow she would be liberated, but today she was sad.

There was a knock at her door, which she figured must be the takeout she had ordered. With her hair up in a messy bun, her feet bare and wearing an oversized T-shirt, Emma went to answer the door, knowing the pizza guy wouldn't care that she looked like a slob.

She pulled the door open, but it definitely wasn't the pizza guy.

'What do you want, Alexander?' she asked. She'd slipped up. Saying his name made her heart skip a beat.

'Can we talk?' he asked hopefully.

Lucky had heard his voice and jumped off the couch to rub himself around Alex's legs.

'Traitor,' Emma mumbled, at her usually aloof cat.

She stood aside, and he picked the cat up as he entered. She went to the couch to get the remote, switching the television off before she faced him.

She wrapped her arms around herself. 'Before you say anything, I want to tell you that you don't need to check up on me. I'm fine. You owe me no explanations. I knew what this was before we started. We're all good.

I'm sure you must be very busy, so you don't have to waste any time here.'

'Can I speak?' Alex asked, and laughed in a defeated way. He put Lucky down on the cushions and took a step towards Emma, but then stopped. 'I do owe you an explanation, Emma, and an apology. I'm here to ask you to forgive me.'

'You're forgiven. You can go now.' She needed him to leave. It was too painful to see him.

'Emma…'

The tormented way he said her name cut right through her.

'Please listen to me, and after that if you still want me to go, I will.'

Emma nodded, and he felt a small amount of relief that she wasn't kicking him out. He still felt as if he was holding in a breath, though. He ran his fingers through his hair, piecing together what he wanted to say.

'I was scared, and I reacted badly.'

A sad smile curved Emma's lips. 'Alex, you don't have to apologise. You told me what you wanted from the start.'

'Please stop calling me Alex,' he begged. 'I do have to apologise—but that's not the only thing. I'm here to tell you I love you.'

'What?' Emma's eyes widened in shock.

'I love you, and I think I have since the first time I met you. I knew you were special then, and I've been scared since that first kiss. I've always had my life ordered just the way I like. You were right. I was always in control because I needed to make sure that *I* was the one who decided who was allowed to enter and leave my life. I could never allow the chaos of love in my life—how could I when I was convinced that I was unlovable?'

Alex closed his eyes and swallowed thickly. Emma could see how hard this was for him.

'Alexander,' she said, reaching for him, and he smiled fleetingly, taking her hand and placing it on his stubbled cheek. 'You could never be unlovable.'

'Of course I could. Why else would a mother leave her child? Why would she know who I am, be in the same room as me, and never once reach out? I wasn't worthy.'

Emma's eyes welled up. 'That's not true. Her decisions don't reflect on who you are.'

'I realise that now, but it made me foolish. It made me hurt you. And I'm so sorry, Emma.' He cradled her face in his hands. 'I didn't want to be falling in love, but I did it anyway. I didn't want to make my father's mistakes and be a broken man when you left, as I was convinced you would.'

Emma couldn't stop the tears that were rolling down her cheeks.

'And when I saw how perfectly you fitted into my life I was terrified, because for the first time I wanted that more than anything. I do want that, Emma. I want to go to sleep with you beside me and wake up with you in my arms. I want to share everything I have, everything I am, with you.'

'Alexander...' she breathed in broken sobs. 'But how do I know you won't get scared again?'

He leaned his forehead against hers, taking a ragged breath. 'I guess you don't. But I promise you I will work every day for the rest of my life to prove myself worthy of you.'

'Worthy of me?'

'Yes! You are the most incredible, courageous, beautiful, intoxicating woman I have ever met. The question is: will you accept me?'

'I love you, Alexander, so much. Of course I accept you! All I want is you.'

'You have me, baby. For the rest of our lives.'

Alex kissed her as he never had before. With desperation and fervency and so much love that neither of them could breathe.

'I have one more thing to ask of you,' he said against her lips. 'Will you and Lucky move in with me?'

Emma laughed brightly, giddy with joy. 'Let's go.'

# EPILOGUE

*Two years later*

THE SKY OVERHEAD was a vibrant blue. Fluffy white clouds drifted over in the gentle breeze that offered some relief from the unusual summer heat. It was a beautiful day. Serene. Even the horses in the paddock seemed to be enjoying the sun.

Emma sat on the red-and-white-checked blanket that was laid on the grass, her back against the trunk of a tree. Fingers stroking through Alex's black hair as he lay with his head in her lap. The sunlight was catching his blue eyes, making them even more vivid than normal. Almost otherworldly.

Emma still couldn't believe that this amazing specimen of a man was hers. He had been for a little over two and a half years now, and in that time so much had changed.

There was no fear of love, nor feelings of inadequacy.

They'd left Melbourne, but travelled back often enough. In fact they travelled extensively, as Alex grew Hastings International. Their most frequent trip was back here, to Greenfield House. A place that Alex had grown to love.

They had come here when he'd proposed to her, in the middle of the maze, when he had set up a scavenger hunt that had ended with him in the centre, waiting on a bended knee. They had come back again when they'd got married in the gardens. And now they were back here for a few days, and intended to stay for a few more.

Alex kissed Emma's swollen belly. He couldn't wait to meet his baby. It had been Emma's idea that they—including Lucky—should spend the pregnancy and the year afterwards in London. She wanted his father to be as close to his grandchild as possible, and Alex had gratefully agreed.

His father had, after all, accepted Emma as the daughter he'd never had, and she'd got the father she always wanted.

Having been back for a few months already, those plans had morphed. They had decided to stay in London permanently. Alex was finally embracing every part of his life. Being heir to an earldom no longer felt like a shackle, and he'd helped Emma set up a British branch of the literacy charity, taking the organisation international—much to Fiona's excitement.

Emma moved the hand that had been in Alex's to her belly. 'Did you feel that?' she asked, and smiled.

Alex beamed. Felt his face lighting up. 'Yes! I can't wait to meet you...' he said, turning over with his lips inches from her belly. 'Take you to your first concert. Teach you how to drive really fast...'

He whispered the last two words, making Emma laugh.

'He's going to be a rower—just like his dad,' she said, kissing her husband on the head.

'He?'

She shrugged. 'I just know. I have a feeling.'

Alex sat up, taking her face in his hands, and kissed her slowly, lovingly. Roving his lips over hers. He couldn't imagine that it was possible to love her any more than he did right now, but he'd thought that the day before, and the day before that. He knew his love for her would only grow. That no matter how much time he had with her it would never be nearly enough.

'I love you, Emma Hastings,' he breathed against her lips.

'I love you too, Alexander.'

* * * * *

## #4049 HER CHRISTMAS BABY CONFESSION
*Secrets of the Monterosso Throne*
by Sharon Kendrick

Accepting a flight home from a royal wedding with Greek playboy Xanthos is totally out of character for Bianca. Yet when they're suddenly snowbound together, Bianca chooses to embrace their deliciously dangerous chemistry, just once...only to find herself carrying a shocking secret!

## #4050 A WEEK WITH THE FORBIDDEN GREEK
by Cathy Williams

Grace Brown doesn't have time to fantasize about her boss, Nico Doukas...never mind how attractive he is! But when she accompanies him on a business trip, the earth-shattering desire between them makes keeping things professional impossible...

## #4051 THE PRINCE'S PREGNANT SECRETARY
*The Van Ambrose Royals*
by Emmy Grayson

Clara is shocked to discover she's carrying her royal boss's baby! The last thing she wants is to become Prince Alaric's convenient princess, but marriage will protect their child from scandal. Can their honeymoon remind them that more than duty binds them?

## #4052 RECLAIMING HIS RUNAWAY CINDERELLA
by Annie West

After years of searching for the heiress who fled just hours after their convenient marriage, Cesare finally tracks Ida down. Intent on finalizing their divorce, he hadn't counted on the undeniable attraction between them! Dare they indulge in the wedding night they never had?

### #4053 NINE MONTHS AFTER THAT NIGHT
*Weddings Worth Billions*
by Melanie Milburne

Billionaire hotelier Jack is blindsided when he discovers the woman he spent one mind-blowing night with is in the hospital... having his baby! Marriage is the only way to make sure his daughter has the perfect upbringing. But only *if* Harper accepts his proposal...

### #4054 UNWRAPPING HIS NEW YORK INNOCENT
*Billion-Dollar Christmas Confessions*
by Heidi Rice

Alex Costa doesn't trust *anyone*. Yet he cannot deny the attraction when he meets sweet, innocent Ellie. Keeping her at arm's length could prove impossible when the fling they embark on unwraps the most intimate of secrets...

### #4055 SNOWBOUND IN HER BOSS'S BED
by Marcella Bell

When Miriam is summoned to Benjamin Silver's luxurious Aspen chalet, she certainly doesn't expect a blizzard to leave her stranded there for Hanukkah! Until the storm passes, she must battle her scandalous and ever-intensifying attraction to her boss...

### #4056 THEIR DUBAI MARRIAGE MAKEOVER
by Louise Fuller

Omar refuses to allow Delphi to walk away from him. His relentless drive has pushed her away and now he must convince her to return to Dubai to save their marriage. But is he ready to reimagine everything he believed their life together would be?

---

**YOU CAN FIND MORE INFORMATION ON UPCOMING HARLEQUIN TITLES, FREE EXCERPTS AND MORE AT HARLEQUIN.COM.**

HPCNMRB0922

SPECIAL EXCERPT FROM

⊕ HARLEQUIN
# PRESENTS

*Cesare intends to finalize his divorce to his runaway
bride, Ida. Yet he hadn't counted on discovering Ida's
total innocence in their marriage sham. Or on the
attraction that rises swift and hot between them...
Dare they indulge in the wedding night they never had?*

*Read on for a sneak preview of
Annie West's 50th book for Harlequin Presents,*
Reclaiming His Runaway Cinderella

"Okay. We're alone. Why did you come looking for me?"

"I thought that was obvious."

How could Ida have forgotten the intensity of that
brooding stare? Cesare's eyes bored into hers as if seeking
out misdemeanors or weaknesses.

But she'd done him no wrong. She didn't owe him
anything and refused to be cowed by that flinty gaze. Ida
shoved her hands deep in her raincoat pockets and raised
her eyebrows.

"It's been a long day, Cesare. I'm not in the mood for
guessing games. Just tell me. What do you want?"

He crossed the space between them in a couple of deceptively easy strides. Deceptive because his expression told her it was the prowl of a predator.

"To sort out our divorce, of course."

"We're still married?"

*Don't miss*
Reclaiming His Runaway Cinderella
*available November 2022 wherever*
*Harlequin Presents books and ebooks are sold.*

Harlequin.com

# Get 4 FREE REWARDS!

**We'll send you 2 FREE Books plus 2 FREE Mystery Gifts.**

FREE
Value Over
**$20**

Both the **Harlequin® Desire** and **Harlequin Presents®** series feature compelling novels filled with passion, sensuality and intriguing scandals.